ALASKA HIGHWAY TWO-STEP

ALASKA HIGHWAY TWO-STEP

CAROLINE WOODWARD

1 2 3 4 5 — 21 20 19 18 17

Lost Moose is an imprint of Harbour Publishing Co. Ltd.
P.O. Box 219, Madeira Park, BC, V0N 2H0
www.harbourpublishing.com

Front cover: Madam Lubouska, dancer, National American Ballet, 1925 from Library of Congress LC-F8- 36237 [P&P]; flowers by lavendertime, Thinkstock; vw dashboard by Uko_Jesita, Thinkstock. Front and back cover: Alaska road by Kevin Russ, Stocksy
Cover design by Anna Comfort O'Keeffe
Text design by Brianna Cerkiewicz
Printed and bound in Canada
Printed on FSC-certified, chlorine-free paper

Excerpts from earlier versions of this novel have appeared in *Dance Connection* and *The Kootenay Review*, and in the short fiction collection *Disturbing the Peace* (Polestar, 1990) by Caroline Woodward.

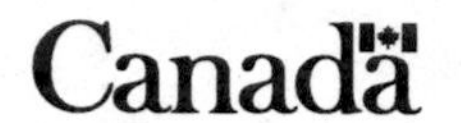

Harbour Publishing acknowledges the support of the Canada Council for the Arts, which last year invested $153 million to bring the arts to Canadians throughout the country. We also gratefully acknowledge financial support from the Government of Canada through the Canada Book Fund and from the Province of British Columbia through the BC Arts Council and the Book Publishing Tax Credit.

LIBRARY AND ARCHIVES CANADA CATALOGUING IN PUBLICATION

Woodward, Caroline, 1952-, author
Alaska highway two-step / Caroline Woodward.

Previously published: Vancouver: Polestar Book Publishers, 1993.
Issued in print and electronic formats.
ISBN 978-1-55017-801-2 (softcover).--ISBN 978-1-55017-802-9 (HTML)

I. Title.

PS8595.O657A79 2017 C813'.54 C2016-907686-5
C2016-907687-3

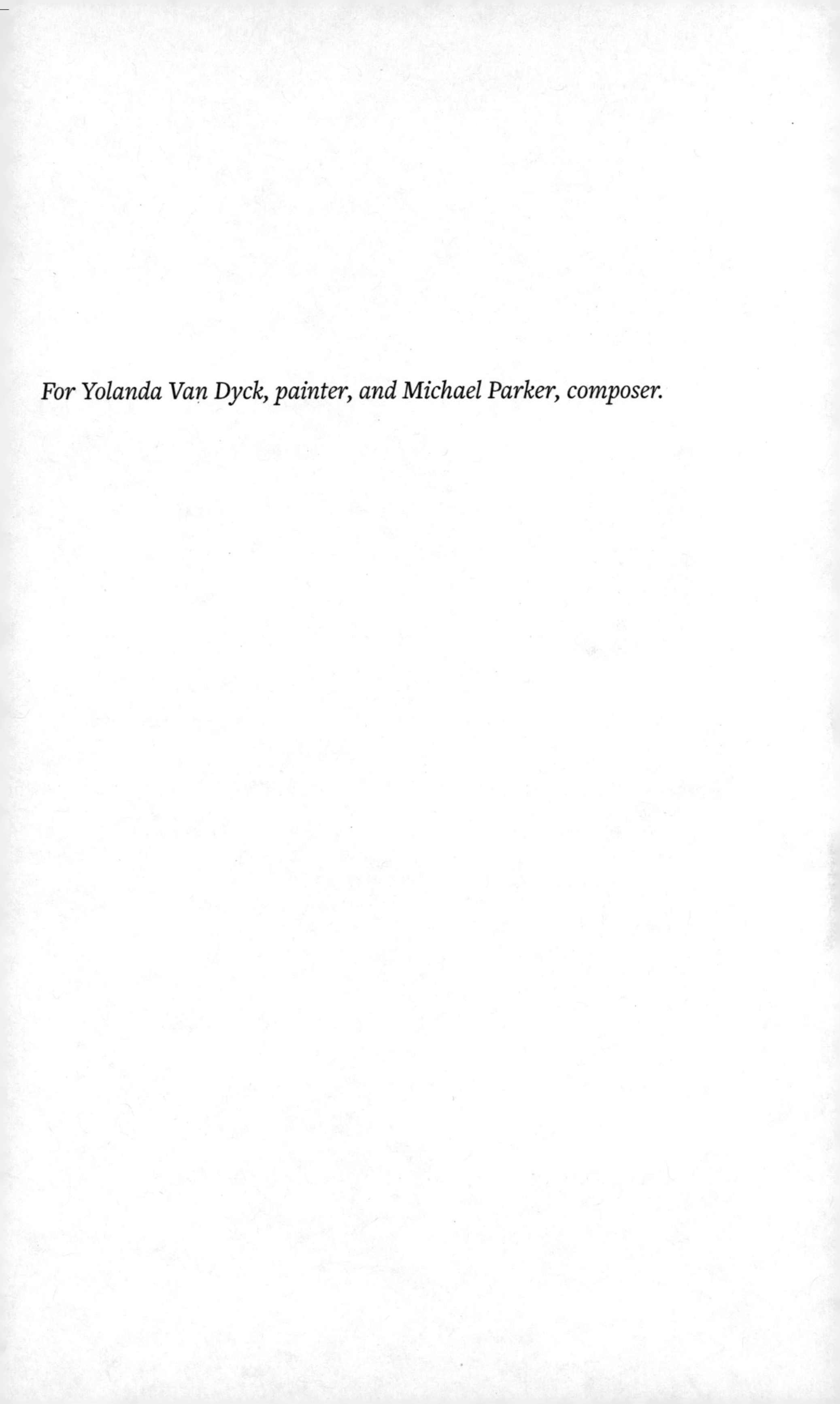

For Yolanda Van Dyck, painter, and Michael Parker, composer.

There was never a place for her in the ranks of the terrible, slow army of the cautious. She ran ahead, where there were no paths.

—Dorothy Parker on Isadora Duncan

A myth is a dream that many have come to tell.

—Amazonian saying

AUTHOR'S NOTE

IN THIS NOVEL, I HAVE incorporated the true story of the Aberfan disaster and a number of accounts by people who had precognitive knowledge of the slide. There is, or was, a British Premonitions Bureau but there is not, to the best of my knowledge, a Canadian or American counterpart. The character of Sadie Brown the dog is as true to life as I can depict. There are also actual, living or dead, dancers named in this novel: Isadora Duncan, Ruth St. Denis, Ted Shawn, Maud Allan, the Royal Winnipeg Ballet, and Judith Marcuse. However, all characters and events and places created in this novel are entirely fictitious or, as in the case of the above-mentioned dancers, used fictitiously.

Acknowledgements

I am very grateful for the Leighton Colony at The Banff Centre, the excellent Banff Library and librarians, and especially Carol Holmes, Jeff Stewart, Fred Truck, and Debbie Rosen for their moral and technical support when my computer crashed repeatedly. I'd also like to thank Verity Purdy and Alanna Matthew, dancers and writers both, for "Ginger" inspiration, Sheila Candy for her Willow Point cottage, Jennie Ash for her roses, Sylvia Dorling, Barb Cruikshank, Linda Cutting, Chris Majka, Joan Webb, Sheilagh Phillips, Meaghan Baxter, Margot Vanderham, Kalene Louise, Rita Moir, and Paulette Jiles for helpful readings, advice, and lively friendship, Mi Woodward for her superb Whitehorse hospitality, Donna MacDonald for her perceptive and encouraging initial editing of this manuscript, Suzanne Bastedo for her careful and caring final edit, Julian Ross and Michelle Benjamin for believing in Mercy's journey, and Kate Walker and Lost Moose for reviving the long-lost travels of Mercy Brown and her canine side-kick! Celestial and actual milk bones to Sadie Brown, Izzy, Beano, Connor, Annie, Skulker, Gator, Pada, Brody, Jessie, Marley, Sam, Taffy, and Harpo for being their doggy selves. And last, but never least, my most grateful thanks to Seamus and Jeff for being patient housemates during a novel.

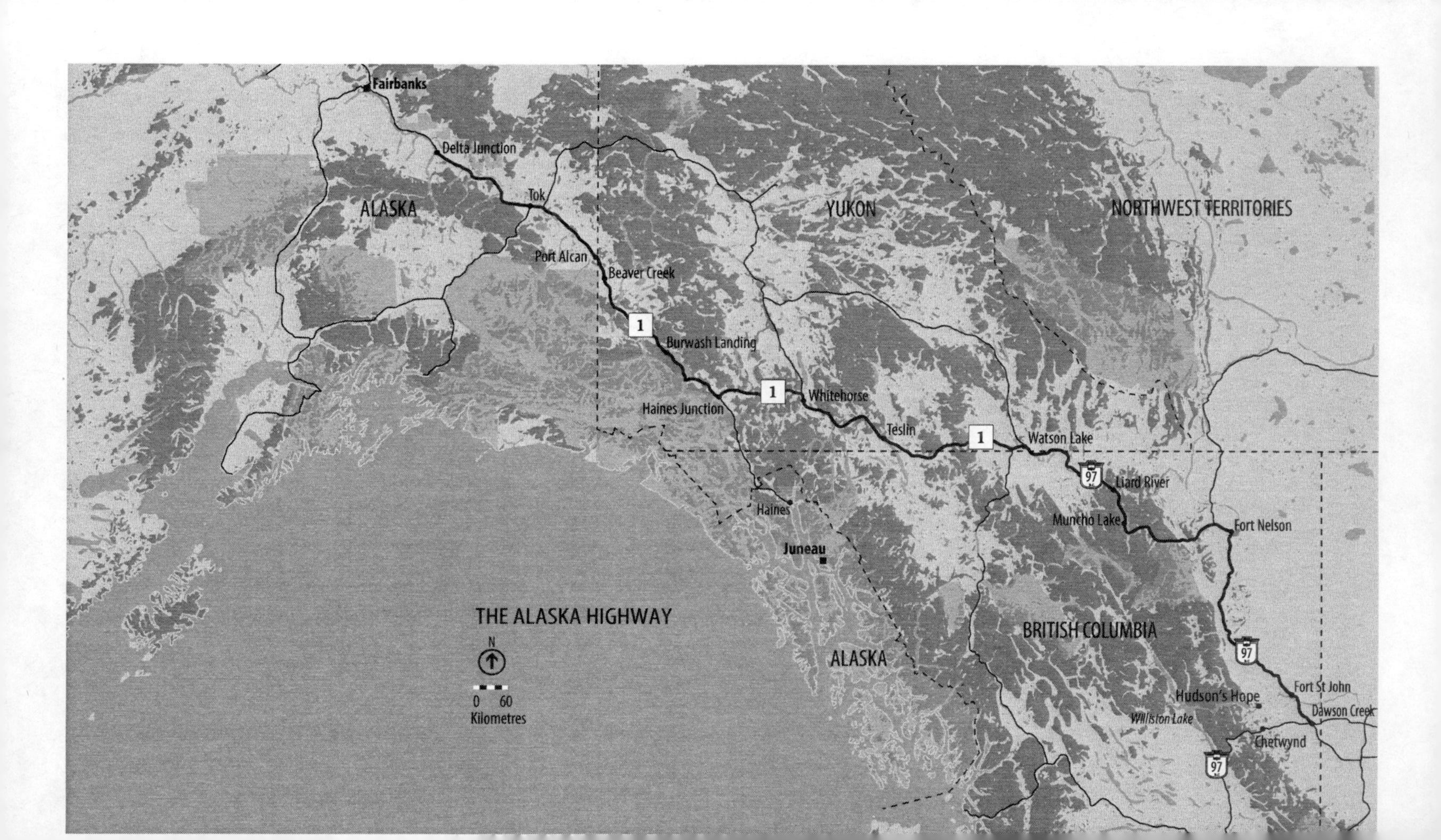
THE ALASKA HIGHWAY
N
0 60
Kilometres
Fairbanks
Delta Junction
Tok
ALASKA
Port Alcan
Beaver Creek
Burwash Landing
Haines Junction
1
YUKON
Whitehorse
Teslin
Haines
Juneau
ALASKA
NORTHWEST TERRITORIES
Watson Lake
97
Liard River
Muncho Lake
Fort Nelson
BRITISH COLUMBIA
Hudson's Hope
Williston Lake
Fort St John
Dawson Creek
Chetwynd

one

NORMAN SZABO SAYS THE MIND is the most temperamental computer ever designed and we don't know the half of it. More like the one one-hundredth of it. Even the tiniest details can add up to the code-breaker. Accumulate the evidence. Be patient. Factor the variables. Analyze the patterns.

But that's his job, not mine. I step into my gumboots, turning them upside down and shaking them first. No spiders, centipedes or moths. Good. I grab the corn broom beside the porch door in one hand and pick up my compost pail in the other.

"Sadie Brown! Sa-a-a-die-e-e!" I bellow melodiously, and wait for the croupy panting and clicking toenails. Here she is, bounding up from the beach, stinking of skunk at ten paces, doggy grin on her chops.

"Right this way, please. Snake alert," I sing out as I clump down the steps to the lower gardens and the compost bin. I stop to usher her past me, encouraging her to scratch and snuffle thoroughly along the path, the better to flush out a pair of greyish garter snakes who've been hanging around the bin. They've taken me by surprise twice now, looking at first glance like long dead sticks, and being so much bigger than the little green and yellow snakes. Even those give me a start and they're rather beautiful and completely harmless. I know these dull ones are harmless too but they have no other redeeming features. Well, okay, they eat mosquitoes and bugs that might get to the garden. True enough But I'm afraid of them and put off going to the compost bin until my household pail begins to overflow with eggshells and coffee grounds.

Sadie turns around at the bin and waits for me. I dump the accumulation of two days' worth of reasonably healthy living except for the burnt rhubarb cobbler. I whip about smartly to get back to the cottage. No sign of the over-sized compost diners today. Good. Freudian clap-trap notwithstanding, snakes give my heart a quick aerobic workout.

The gardens need some work soon but I can't get at it today, not with this hot springs article due by four o'clock. The daffodils bob in the small, chilly breezes coming in off the lake. The massed plantings of grape hyacinths look glorious next to the two-tone yellows of the daffy, my early red tulips and the ancient border of purple heather. The blue spruce trees on either side of the long lane leading up to the highway have bright green new needles on the tips of their dark branches. Best of all, the long line of fifty-year-old rhododendrons on the south side of this place look like they'll be in full bloom in just a week or ten days. Masses of blossoms as big as dinner plates: pale antique orange, bright fuchsia, shell pink, light purple, scarlet red with white centres...

Aunt Ginger, bless her, always had the Rosemont Painters out in the spring for the rhodies and it seems I am expected to keep the tradition going, not that I mind. I use her very best Spode china and I make sure to use No. 1 Ceylon from the trunk she brought back from Sri Lanka on her last world tour. The Painters bring dainty baked specialties to eat so I am let off the hook as far as cooking is concerned. Last year I dressed up in one of Aunt Ginger's rayon floral dresses and sent the Painters into a major twittering backspin.

"Just then...when you brought out the tea tray...on the porch... the very image!...She wore that exact dress in early spring, if I'm not mistaken...Ginger's niece, you know, the others all married, I believe...Why, thank you, Mercy, your Aunt Ginger would be pleased that you used her good china for our little group!" and on and on like that. Lovely ladies painting together for over thirty years, twice a month, with a Spring Colours show (I get a special invitation to that because my rhododendrons are the main feature) and a Fall Splendour show at the Rosemont Gallery.

I haven't bothered hemming her dresses because I wear them just below mid-calf whereas Aunt Ginger, at nearly six feet, strode around like the daughter of the twenties that she was, with her terrific dancer legs and her skirts grazing her muscular knee-caps. I'm almost a foot shorter than she was but we share, unfortunately, the no-nonsense Brown beak and an adventurous streak that made us both unfit for conventional employment or marriage. Still, I wish I'd inherited her legs as well as this schnozz and her beautiful old place.

Not that we're unsociable or willfully eccentric. We both like parties and travelling and pitching in for community events and assorted good causes. But I absolutely must have peace and quiet, daily hours of solitude, to keep sane, and I think Aunt Ginger must have needed that too. Why else would she have lived alone for over sixty years?

beauty and truth, truth and beauty,
we believe in these above all

Who...? Sadie? Oh, there you are, good girl! Brrr. It's nippy enough with the winds coming in off the lake. I feel a tad melancholy, this raw spring weather, an assignment I'm sick and tired of rewriting, no slush fund to tap for a quick two-day getaway to a nice little bed and breakfast with a stack of books to read...or, better yet, I could spend the whole day out here in my gumboots grey sweats and old red Hudson's Bay coat, grubbing in the good earth. But. No. Mercy Brown has bills to pay and a dog to feed The day will come when I can putter around in the gardens with not a care in the world except having enough bone meal on hand Right now "Hot springs of the Pacific Northwest" needs a final edit, a new lead paragraph and cutlines for five photographs.

I clump back up the slate footpath, stop to pick several brown lilac blossoms from the bushes flanking the porch steps and then, I can't help myself, I have to inspect the roses. Aunt Ginger planted antique shrub roses and climbers along the west side of the cottage. Whenever I open the bedroom windows in summer, the fragrance of the roses overwhelms me. I regularly swoon, all by myself unfortunately, on the king-sized four-poster bed, thanks to Apothecary's Rose, Cardinal De Richelieu, Duchesse De Montebello and the divine Moonlight.

Last spring, two months after I moved in, my friend Terry went under the knife for breast cancer and a vast network of family and friends is now waiting out the five-year prognosis. Somehow I got it in my head to plant a rose especially for Terry—if a rose could live through five years, then Terry would too. I dislike this quirk I have of attaching omens to things. I try very hard to squelch such mental aberrations but the harder I squelch, the more firmly rooted becomes the silly superstition. So I drove two hundred kilometres to find the antique rose nursery where Aunt Ginger often went, only to discover that the owners had retired. Luckily for me, they still lived next to the nursery. These tiny transplanted Welshmen with their bushy white mops of hair were happy to see me; they had been big fans of Aunt Ginger.

"Smashing woman, knew what she was about...Indeed she did, loved our roses she did...So very sorry, eighty-three was she?... Indeed I am as well, a good age though?"

Then they tottered out to their own garden and came back with a two-year-old Thérèse Bugnet in a large clay pot and wouldn't hear of my paying for it.

"Think of it as our little commemoration for your auntie. Yes, please do take it, the very least we can do."

> A hybrid rugosa bred in Canada in 1950 with fragrant lilac-pink blooms on a tall and healthy shrub, the first and last to bloom and absolutely untouched by winter.

So reads Ms. Bugnet's catalogue description, making her entirely apt as a talisman of my hopes for Terry and as a commemoration of Aunt Ginger. I drove back home in the dark, feeling a strange mixture of fondness for my aunt and helpless dread for my friend.

Now, the rose looks awfully stark to me—three small dark brown branches protruding from the mulch with not a leaf in sight. The rest of the roses look much the same. I shouldn't worry. Last spring, I'd come around the corner after being away for the first two weeks of May, and they were bursting out all over in lime green buds and leaves. They're probably just being very sensible about fickle April weather. I'm being very

needlessly superstitious in this case
but pay attention to the other

What? Who's there? I didn't hear anybody drive down the lane unless it's Corey coming by to see if there are any odd jobs to do..."Hello? I'm by the house!"

Huh. Nobody. Weird glitch in my ears. Well, enough of this. It's very ill-disciplined of me to stand here wishing there was just one late-blooming lilac left for me to sniff. The essence of spring for me—lilacs and the warm sun on my back, clouds of generous, sweet lilacs in every room. I'd meander from vase to bowl, sinking my big, sharp schnozz into white and purple flowerets like an adoring giant, a human bee. Yes!

No. I must get straight to work before I send down roots myself Lash, lash, back to work, two solid hours, then I play!

TWO

THIS, THEN, MAKES LIFE WORTH living. The late afternoon sun shines onto the deck where I'm protected from the lake winds, nestled in my old down mummy bag on a wicker chaise lounge. Beside me, a pot of Earl Grey tea and a tray of arrowroot biscuits, a little stale, it's true, but just fine for dunking.

If someone were to come around the corner, I'm sure I'd look like a contented green larva wearing a beret and sunglasses. The sun won't last much longer but the hot springs assignment is out of my hair so I can finally relax. It's too early to panic about where my next paycheque is coming from. I've learned how important it is for a freelance writer to enjoy the completion of a task well done, even to make a ritual out of so humble an event as tea and biscuits and an undisturbed hour in a sleeping bag. I can't afford Hawaii or even Mexico. This is a mini-holiday for me, to doze in this honey-coloured sunlight with only the voices of lake gulls and a squirrel for company and the faraway drone of a truck downshifting on the highway. S.B. heaves a big sigh and stretches out below me. My lungs fill up with a big whiff of lake water and cottonwood sap. Heaven on earth, yes indeed, heaven...

The big Balm of Gilead rolls toward her, half its leaves and branches underwater and its huge clump of roots covered with dirt, small rocks and grass. Her breathing hurts, big ragged gasps, her arms flail at what looks like a branch. The tree rolls again. She finds one foot wedged in some of its unseen branches. She kicks free, grabbing onto a big branch dripping with muddy river water. She gropes her way along the trunk stepping underwater most of the way. The tree must be thirty metres long! It seems to be slipping sideways into a backwater, no, a small dead-end canyon with steep shale cliffs rising up. She looks up, sees a maroon truck, 1950s vintage with a gleaming paint job, tilting nose down into the saskatoon bushes, dangerously close to the cliffs. A man in a green workshirt slumps over the steering wheel.

"Look out!" shrieks a dirty white gull perching on top of the roots.

"Mind yer own damn business!" squawks another who lands beside the first one.

She looks up at the cliffs again to find the truck but she has to concentrate on hanging on as the tree starts a sickening sideways roll, the upper end of its leaves and branches sucked back into the main current, its clump of roots an anchor in the backwaters. Then she sees the police cruiser and two people, a woman and a man in khaki uniforms, passing binoculars between them directly across the small coulee from the crashed truck. The man inside the truck is beginning to move but they're looking at her, not at him.

"Truck! Crash!" she shouts, using her left hand to point at the truck. The binoculars stay fixed in her direction.

"Truck, there!" she yells again, as the man in the maroon truck starts to crawl out the driver's side window and collapses.

The tree trunk straightens out and she has to use both hands to grab on as it picks up speed. Ahead, there is nothing but brown water, wide as a lake, filled with uprooted trees like hers and big chunks of ice. The riverbanks rise up steeply through a misty green haze of trees and bushes.

Beside her swims a green and yellow garter snake, a puzzled look on its petite reptile face. She straddles the tree trunk and leans over to pick up the snake at the place where its neck should be. It goes limp. She places it gently in front of her on the massive trunk where it busies itself into a neat coil with its head looking her way and its tiny forked tongue hanging off to one side.

"Thank you, you really didn't need to do that but I'm truly grateful," says the snake, in a voice belonging to Aunt Ginger. She/it heaves a wheezy sigh of relief. All those slim port cigarillos.

The tree starts to roll again and she and the snake exchange startled looks. She climbs to her feet, crouching over like a circus horse rider. Two deer swim past, a doe and a young buck with velvet horns, eyes flashing white. They are all heading for a steep bank, which the river is carving away in big chunks. The deer reach it first, their shining black hooves daintily battering at the cutbank, trying to gain a foothold. The bank keeps caving in. The river sucks them back away from the land and she starts to scream now, feeling the icy water for the first time, feeling trapped by something relentless. Her tree smashes into another tree, an even larger one. Her wretched knees lock instead of buckling to absorb the impact and then, oh no, she pitches forward into the cold blackness.

I smash my head on the teapot, spilling lukewarm liquid down my neck. My arms are trapped and so are my legs. Sleeping bag. I remember now. I extract my left arm and roll away from the spilled tea and crushed biscuits on the floor beside the chaise lounge. Good grief. I finally pry myself out of the sleeping bag and head for the porch door, tripping on the compost pail and knocking over the tin watering can half-full of diluted Alaska fish fertilizer.

"No!" I wail and haul myself up, reaching for the mop in the far corner of the deck. Sadie Brown jumps around me and sticks her nose into the smelly brown stuff and is about to take an experimental slurp.

"No!" I screech at her. "Get out of it, go on!" She slinks around to the armchair on the deck. "Get off that chair!" I yell. She claws the screen door open and scuttles into the cottage.

I mop up and go out on the deck. I plop down on the wicker armchair, to recover and to apologize to my dog.

"Come here, darling dog," I warble soothingly. No toenails clicking on hardwood floors.

"S.B., I'm sorry, come here and I'll give you a paw massage." After several long seconds I hear a series of subdued clicks, then the squeak of the screen door. She is holding the door open with her nose and giving me a reproachful sidelong look. I use both palms to beat out an enthusiastic drum roll on my knees. Even this does not move her.

"Come here, best buddy, I done you wrong, I bamboozled my brain with a big, bad bang, I butter you up bountifully for being such a bag!"

All the "b" words are her favourites—don't ask me why—and I succeed with this big batch of them. She pads over, tail still tucked under in disgrace mode.

I hug her with gusto, skunk smell and all. The cider vinegar anti-skunk rinse and herbal dog shampoo compete for olfactory points. True to my word, I deliver a paw massage. Shiatsu for canines. I really should patent it, write a book. People would line up in droves to buy it. Full colour illustrations. *How-To Shiatsu For Your Familiar And You.* S.B. pants happily. A dog smile returns to her long black lips and the eyes I adore return my loveshine a hundred-fold.

This is not the first time I've encountered the floating tree, the flooding river or the squawking gulls. I think I dreamt some of it last night too. This whole scenario feels very fresh. I don't like this movie. I don't care to see how it ends, thank you very much. But I'd better send it up to Norman. It's a live one.

THREE

I LOOK AT THE SCREEN, scroll through the two-page report for Norman Szabo one more time and send it off.

In less than five minutes, my phone rings. "Hiya, Norman," I say.

"Yikes! You're really getting good at this stuff!" A small amount of static interferes with the wires from Whitehorse but there is no mistaking the bass rumble of Norman Joe Szabo.

"Nah, you know I'm the ultra-rational type, eh? I figured if you were home from work by six o'clock, chances were very good I'd hear from you pronto."

"Yes, ma'am. You're the third report in today, two yesterday and...I've got another one on the go here."

Norman is the only person in the world who calls me "ma'am" besides store clerks who size me up and figure, quite rightly, that I'm past the "May I help you, Miss?" stage of life. But with Norman, it's okay. It makes me feel like Miss Kitty to his Matt Dillon. I've never met Norman except via our correspondence and the telephone. He's got a great voice.

"Mercy? Are you still there? Can you hear me?" The great voice is talking. The great daydreamer wafts back to earth.

"Yes, I'm here. Sorry."

"Okay, good. Now, I'm just curious. Is this one a night incident or daytime?"

"Both, I'm fairly certain of that. How many did you say had called in?"

"Six so far. It could be an isolated flurry, except you and two of the others are in my Top Ten list of receivers, so I'm taking it very seriously. It could be the advance guard for a big one somewhere."

"Or we could be the mop-up crew reporting after the fact. Do you get much of that?" I blat out, and immediately wish I'd stifled myself. I might come across as terminally skeptical.

"That does happen and it's a real hazard. People watch the late night news, fall asleep, have bad dreams about God knows what, I mean, look at the material they're crunching through. Then they send me material that turns out to be El Salvador's death squads, some creepo killing prostitutes in Vancouver or a political assassination in Beirut. But like I say, better to stay on top of it all, know the late night news when you see it, than to dismiss something important. So, can you give me a few seconds here to get set up and we'll do a tape?"

"Sure, ready anytime you are," I say.

He's smart and tactful too. Always explains things. Most things. During the Nitassinan work, I resisted everything, asked questions constantly. Not only had I felt isolated, but too much depended on these annoying, frightening, utterly vivid dreams of mine. Norman patiently explained his computer network and the three-hundred-plus people hooked into it. People like me. Five months later, the low-flying military harassment of so-called uninhabited Nitassinan stopped, with a United Nations edict in place, no thanks to the duplicitous mealy-mouthing of the government. Norman says he can't talk about some of it. Sworn to secrecy. National security. Uh huh. That's why I'm still skeptical about all this stuff. Still...

trust yourself listen up you're not demented, girl!

"Sorry? Norman? I didn't catch that last bit."

"I wasn't saying anything. Ready to go?"

"Yes," I say, feeling a bit weebly. Weebly? "Hold on just a second, okay?" I cushion the phone against the sofa to muffle the sound of my next question. *That* word is not *my* word. I know exactly whose word it is and whose word it has been for eighty-five years, give or take a year. Though *she* probably catapulted from the womb of Great-Grandmother Grace talking a blue streak from the get-go.

"Aunt Ginger! Is that you?" I croak, clear my throat and quickly scan the living room crammed with her 1920s mohair sofas, overstuffed chairs, and Tiffany lamps. Sadie Brown thumps her tail on the floor and whines softly. Nothing else shakes, rattles or rolls. I turn back to the phone, pick it up and walk over to the bay window overlooking the lake.

"Norman? Ready anytime," I say, in a loud, firm voice. What a faker!

"Okay, I'm all set here now. Let's do a run-through of the elements, beginning with the tree in the water," says Norman, encouraging, professional, utterly unaware that I am dealing with weirdness everywhere I turn.

"Tree. Poplar or black poplar. Medicinal sap, smells a bit like cottonwood. Balm of Gilead. That's another name for it."

"As in the hymn? 'There is a balm in Gilead'?" sings Norman, completely unselfconsciously and very nicely, too.

"Yes! You sing?"

"The Whitehorse Choral Society, two concerts a year. Depend on us for Bach's *Magnificat* and Handel's *Messiah,* on alternate years at Christmas. CBC Radio tapes us and out we go on the airwaves to Faro and Old Crow and Inuvik and all points in between. This year we're going on the new northern television program as well. As long as there are more than two others singing bass, I can belt it out with confidence. Now, where are we? Gulls. Please go on to the gulls, Mercy."

"Gulls!" I blurt. I have to get focused. "Gulls, talking birds. Yes. Rude, jeering types, like the kind of people I try to avoid at all costs. Noisy, belligerent, too stubborn and stupid to know they're unbearable to be around. I know that's just a tad judgmental but these gulls get my adrenaline up. I'm always at a loss almost tongue-tied, when I have to deal with blatant rudeness and mean-spiritedness. I just can't comprehend how anyone can live with themselves after spending the day dumping on everybody else—quite literally, in the case of gulls."

"The snake?" Norman is snickering and I am suddenly pleased.

"A small, pretty garter snake, green and yellow. You know, I have a bit of a phobia about snakes. Actually, more like a full-fledged phobia. But this one, in the water, looked so puzzled and confused and that's how I felt too, just watching this bizarre movie or dream-thing, vision, whatever...Anyway, I picked the snake up. It wasn't slimy or anything, just warm and alive! Aren't snakes cold-blooded? Doesn't matter. I'm trying to be rational. Okay, so, the snake was ever so dainty."

"Your preliminary report says, 'Thank you, you really didn't need to do that but I'm truly grateful,' and then you have a question mark and 'Voice? Ginger?' What's that? You lost me there."

This is the part that gets me feeling foolish. "I thought the snake talked like my Aunt Ginger," I say, trying for an airy, noncommittal tone.

"Really? Didn't you move into your aunt's place last year, just before the Nitassinan work?"

"Yes. What do you think of that? I wish I knew what this stuff meant! Norman, get real now. Is any of this any use at all?" I feel like a fanciful nitwit all over again.

"Absolutely. I'm sure of it. You're in my Top Ten, remember, you're a top-notch sensor even though you try to deny it. Stay open-minded about all of it. If it helps you to feel useful, just remember Nitassinan. Between you and the other four sensors, we had the place pin-pointed on the map because you picked up the landforms, the bird migration route and the two rivers joining up. Trust yourself! You're doing a good job! Now, ready for more?"

Trust yourself. *She* would say that, striding around tapping cigarillo ash in the general direction of the standing ashtrays and swooping her right arm around to make her points even more forceful and expansive. Aunt Ginger was an Isadora Duncan fan and she, too, must have dominated every stage she was on, all swirling silks and bare feet.

"Yo! I'm not exactly sharp as a tack, sorry to say. But yes, let's keep at it. Deer?"

"May as well do all the wildlife first. Go ahead," he says.

"Two. Young male, bigger doe, maybe mother and son. Frightened. Trying to get out of the water. I think they're going to drown. God, how awful, but it's true. They know it, too."

"Yeah, they sense it all right. We should have as much sense as they do," Norman blurts out with feeling. "Three of the reports have animals drowning! It's upsetting to say the least. In Nitassinan the jets drove animals over cliffs, among other things. Now these drowning reports! I don't know which is worse but I fear water like some people fear flying."

"Or snakes," I say, inanely. What am I trying to do here? One-up Norman in the phobia department? Anyway, I don't think I'm afraid of snakes anymore. "Norman? What's next?"

"Landforms, Mercy. What did it look like out there on the log? Think left, right, up and down. Go."

"At first, the canyon, really just a recess of, oh, less than one hundred metres from the river. Shale, steep sides. Flat top. In the main channel, on either side the land is flat, like a plateau. There are cutbanks, yellowish colour. I remember trees, but they were far away, beautiful gleaming white tree trunks with leaves that are that fresh lime green of spring. It must have smelled wonderful It's a rip-off not being able to smell during these, whatever they are, even though smells in my regular life send me off to other planets!" Good grief! I am blushing madly, thinking of roses Why can't I just shut up? I'm becoming one of those unfortunate people who can't stop talking, the kind other people roll their eyes about and invent boiling kettles for after five minutes on the phone.

"Good work, Mercy. Plateaus, eh? That fits. Now, the water."

Just the facts ma'am. Button up except for the facts. "Muddy, full of floating debris, big hunks of ice, all sorts of trees, evergreens, poplars. Very strong current. It's..."

"Yes?" asks Norman.

"Odd. That's what it is. The tree keeps getting sucked out by the current and swung around a lot, and it rolls a lot, but...the current isn't right somehow. Up ahead, now I remember, up ahead the water is coming in big rolling waves and there are whitecaps and all that deadhead junk in the water. It's no place to be is what I'm trying to say. Yet the log is moving forward to meet this wall of waves. The current is going in two directions! I'm not even going to try and *think* my way through this lot! You go figure!"

"Very interesting, this is a new one. Good work. Now, the people, please."

"Okay," I say, feeling back on track again. "The man in the maroon truck has on a workshirt, a shade of muted green. Some men wear pants the same colour? Hard-wearing cloth. Lots of farmers wear that kind. Anyway, he's slumped over the wheel, one arm is slung over the wheel and his head must be near the window. I can't see his face. It's an immaculate old truck with those big curving fenders and a silver grill. I like that old-fashioned maroon colour but I'm no expert on makes and models, sorry."

"No problem. And the others, the police with the binoculars?"

"Too far away to get a better description. I saw the flash of the sun on the glass first. They were passing the binoculars back and forth. I wish I could say more but there you have it."

"And the end of it? Can you go a little further?"

"The end. Well. I'm looking at my copy here and all I get is the feeling of a stupid mistake, the knees betraying the body, the truly sickening feeling of something solid giving out from underfoot, the biting coldness of the water. The blackness is similar to fainting. And then I hit my head."

"You don't have that here! You hit your head?" Norman sounds pleased again.

"I mean to say, the nasty little movie ended and I came to on my deck, denting my skull on my teapot and then I tripped." I need to stop talking like this. The Canadian Bureau of Premonitions is *not* interested in my clumsiness, in the line of duty or not.

"But, Mercy, your head is okay?"

"Yes. I have a dent and a sore spot and a bluish line across my forehead but I'll survive. Now, you'll let me know if anything comes of this?"

"Surely. Aha, something else is coming in! Whiskey Jack. He's another live one. Better go. Thanks again for all of this. I'll be in touch. Bye."

And then Norman's gone, the line is dead and I've had my thrill for the day.

don't be silly! the world is your oyster
if you don't hide under your shell you know

"Aunt Ginger, come right out wherever you are! Don't take potshots at me. It's not fair!"

I am shaking with fear and trying for a determined, angry effect now, ready to have it out with that ancient flapper, that octogenarian black sheep.

And there she sits on the burgundy divan. Dyed black bob, hooded green eyes with Rudolph Valentino makeup, the silk teal-green dance dress we cremated her in. She crosses the famous legs and lights a lean brown cigarillo. And smiles her most winning smile. I must have bitten my tongue when I fainted

FOUR

SADIE BROWN LICKS MY FACE and whimpers and nudges at me. I am on the Persian carpet, the one some prince gave to you-know-who after seeing her dance in some tent in the Moroccan desert. I now have the opportunity to study the pattern closely and I find it pleasing to the eye. Little lions and fish and birds. Gold and turquoise and a deep, dark red.

"I'm okay, S.B.," I manage, finally.

The phone rings and I am momentarily confused as the ringing in my ears competes for attention. I stick out my tongue and touch the bitten part with my finger. My elbows must have taken the brunt of this tumble because they are fiery with pain. I can't take much more of this. I get up on my hands and knees and trundle over to the phone while S.B. howls pitifully.

"Stop it! It's the phone!" I say this to her every time the phone rings more than twice and I've been saying this for nine years to no avail.

"Hello?" I say in a rickety voice I barely recognize.

"May I speak with Mercy Brown please?" A brisk, pleasant-sounding woman's voice.

"This is she," I say, automatically reaching for my pen and note pad and discreetly clearing my throat.

"Lona Garrison of *Great Northwest Expeditions* here. I'm replacing Bronwen Williams who's on leave for three months She suggested I get in touch with you about a feature issue for the magazine. It's about the Alaska Highway, Dawson Creek to Fairbanks, which we'd like to send you up to cover."

"Well, that sounds interesting! What's the deadline?" I try to sound brisk and pleasant myself. I feel like whooping with unrestrained glee!

"First of August. Can you manage that? We'd want you to drive down from Fairbanks to Dawson Creek and to take the BC Ferries boat up, connecting with an Alaska State Ferry in Prince Rupert, docking in Haines, Alaska. We booked passage a year ago, so it's confirmed from Port Hardy for June first."

"Sounds fine!" I chirp. "It's been a while since I hit the road for a good, long stretch. I'm looking forward to going up that far north. I've only been up as far as Prince Rupert."

"Good to hear. You'll recall our Spring issue was entirely devoted to the anniversary of the building of the Alaska Highway. It generated so much interest that we decided to follow up with more northern feature issues. So, we'd like you to give us a variety of human settlements, from isolated cabins to the big cities, any wild river stories you can deliver and...oh, okay, Ed wants me to tell you he really likes the hot springs article you just filed and he says there are some nifty hot springs up there too. Does this resemble hard work yet?" She sounds nice. I'm glad they have somebody good to fill Bronwen's shoes.

"It sounds like the ideal assignment, thank you very much!"

"Thank you for taking this on, Mercy. We know you'll do a great job. 'A fine photojournalist in one energetic package' is how Bronwen described you! I'll send your press pass, the contract and supporting materials by courier today. Feel free to call us, if you have any questions at all. Bye now."

I must remember to thank Bronwen for recommending me for this. Heck, I'll wire her some flowers. This is big-time for me. *Great Northwest Expeditions* pays just one rung below *National Geographic.* Two assignments from them in one year! At last, a decent stretch of well-paid work instead of having to slave over short newspaper pieces that take me nearly as much time to research as full-length articles. I'm lucky to break even on those if I value my time at all, and I do.

I don't want to sit on the divan where I hallucinated Aunt Ginger. I flop into the big olive-green mohair armchair, switch on the lamp beside me and sink into the most comfortable chair in the world.

"Sadie B., we are living in interesting times, old thing," I say, scratching behind her ears with my left hand. I stick out my tongue to see if I can still locate my bite mark. At this rate of self-inflicted physical abuse, I am likely to drown in my evening bath. Fear of bathtubs. Drainophobic? Hydrophobic? Mercy, get a grip.

I'll have to make a list for this trip. Yes, that's what I'll do. Nothing like a nice tidy list to settle a person down.

Van
tune-up, oil change
rotate tires, decide on spares (check specials at shops)
stove fixed and hooked up
ditto for fridge
wire mesh to protect headlights
new exhaust and muffler system
Total est. $650-$750

Work Gear
tape recorder, tapes, batteries
camera and bulk film
all the usual/notebooks/pens

maps, *The Milepost* guide to the Alaska Highway, compass
laptop, etc.
sketch book, pencils, charcoals

Food Supplies
40 kg kibble
30 tins of S.B.'s canned food
2 extra insulin
90 needles
90 dog biscuits
30 noodle dinners
30 herbs'n'butter rice pkg.
10 kg 7-grain cereal
5 kg powdered milk
2 kg demerara sugar
5 pkg. coffee
Earl Grey, mint, rosehip tea bags
24 tins mushroom soup
24 tins salmon
24 tins sardines
24 cans 2% milk
12 packs of rye crisp
popcorn
spices, engevita yeast, oyster sauce
dried soup mix (bulk)
1 pkg parmesan cheese
12 cans garbanzos
12 cans kidney beans
12 cans each green & yellow beans
olive oil, salad oil
apple cider & red wine vinegar

Clothing Supplies
blue suit

black suit
yellow rain gear
sweats and jeans
windbreaker
socks, underwear
swimming gear
2 cotton sundresses
old black sweater
plaid bush shirt
several T-shirts
one snazzy outfit
slippers, runners, bush boots, sandals, beige pumps, black pumps

Miscellaneous
health food store mosquito dope
make sure S.B.'s rabies shot still good re: U.S. border crossing
dry clean sleeping bag
hold mail May 15-July 15
pay Corey to mow lawn l/week
call Terry, Mike, Hope, Faith, George, Dr. Swanson
binoculars
kayak & gear
extra windshield fluid
vitamins
2 bottles of Chardonnay, 1 Irish Mist
10 bottles of no-name mineral water (large)
check condition of plates, bowls, etc. take the good pots & pans
S.B.'s travel bowls, leash, long line, basket, kitty litter

There! I always feel better after a good stint of list-making. As long as I can tick off my lists, I have the most comforting illusion that everything is under control. I'll have enough food to eat a monotonous but nourishing diet even if a bridge on the highway washes out and I have to wait for a crew to replace it. I'll buy fresh veggies and fruit en route and, I hope, some salmon and halibut

Now I'll tempt the Fates and run a nice bath with my special no-cruelty-to-little-bunny-eyes bath oil. Better put some nice bath and shower stuff on the list too. Nothing like a bit of pampering in a motel bathtub after a long stretch of driving and camping

I'm just drifting off to sleep when I remember the rhododendron painting bee. I sit up straight. Will I delay my most lucrative and exciting freelance assignment to host the Rosemont Painting Club? Will the rhododendrons appear in good time and spare me the stress of making this decision? Will a spell of hot spring weather solve all my problems? We'll have to see. It's not on my list. Not to worry. There's not a thing I can do about it. Good night.

good night little worry wart

?...

FIVE

I WAKE UP FROM A long, dreamless sleep and start coffee proceedings in my tiny perfect kitchen. Sun splashes over the peach and ivory walls and cupboards I painted in February. The new day out there looks glorious, not a cloud in the sky. My nose appreciates the spring perfume of cottonwood buds.

I remember fretting about the rhododendrons last night and feel reassured. If this weather keeps up, I'll phone the Rosemont Painters tomorrow to give them a week's notice. There are already flashes of colour in the wall of green over there.

The dense stand of cottonwoods and spruce immediately behind the two-metre-high rhododendrons continues for a quarter of a mile along the lake, giving this cottage the ultimate in privacy. Towering red sandstone cliffs immediately to the south are unbuildable terrain and they force the highway well back, muffling the sound of traffic. My cream-coloured cottage with chocolate-brown trim and cedar shake roof nestles between the cliffs and the trees on its own red sand beach. The floating boathouse is painted to match the cottage.

One of the moral obligations of Aunt Ginger's will was that the property remain intact. No subdivision into a row of monster houses crammed side by side, each with twenty metres of waterfront. Fine by me. The compromise we reached before her death was that my sisters and brother, Faith, Hope and Justice, could build their own guest cabins among the trees.

This is a family project we look forward to. In fact, Faith and her husband, Thomas, and the kids are coming this July. Oh no, I'll be away! I'll phone them today; they're on my list. They can just take over this cottage. That's fine. And we'll visit in the last half of July while I pound out the Alaska Highway articles. Oh dear. I can't work with a bunch of people around. No, I've got to have it to myself for the writing. The polishing up, nips-and-tucks stage of it. Oh dear, what to do? I am counting on holing up in a motel somewhere in the Yukon and doing most of the work while it's still fresh in my mind. I can verify my research reasonably quickly and cheaply, too. Cut down on the long-distance calls. Yes, I'll find a nice motel beside a little river and just go at it.

I stand on the deck with my one permitted morning coffee and look at the lake, which is in its Silvery Blue Mirror state. There's no such thing as a bad day beside this lake. Even the storms, especially the storms, are wonderful to watch from inside a cozy house. I'll be seeing lots of new lakes in the north. I look forward to getting my kayak on as many of them as possible. But now I have to make my phone calls, write my notes, go into town. May as well buy my non-perishable supplies and get the van booked into the garage.

The hot springs article payment will certainly come in handy for new tires and some of the other necessities. I will definitely need to dip into what's left of my savings to front the money for the rest of my transportation and supplies. No! I'm going to ask the magazine to advance me a couple of thousand dollars. Surely I'm credible enough for them to risk that much on me. Yes, that's what I'll do. What's left of my savings is my life raft between assignments. It's kibble and insulin for my half-blind, diabetic dog and sardines on crackers and café au 2 percent lait for me.

SIX

THE ROSEMONT PAINTERS WILL BE here by one o'clock. I've ironed another of Aunt Ginger's terrific rayon dresses, all violet and lilac colours, and I've outdone myself and made five dozen coconut macaroons.

"Oh you shouldn't have!" they'll all tut-tut before diving on them like so many silver-haired, sweet-voiced chickadees. I'm looking forward to them, I guess because they're one last link with Aunt Ginger. The weather has co-operated beautifully and the rhododendrons are absolutely magnificent, at their multicoloured peak.

I'd better change into the tea dress at the very last minute. Knowing me, I'll slop something on it or catch it on a nail. Now, the tea. None left in the caddy in the kitchen. Nothing but the best, tip-top leaves of the tea plant, Ceylon No. 1, for our Rosemont Painters.

I'll have to head downstairs to Aunt Ginger's collection of trunks. Downstairs. Shudder. Spider and newt territory. As long as the gas furnace, which I replaced just last fall, keeps going and the water pipes don't freeze, I really don't care if I ever have to go down there. The only storage space in this little three-room cottage, however, is downstairs, and downstairs I must go.

I brace my feet and heave at the brass ring to lift the trap door in the hallway. Damp, cool, stagnant air plumes upward. I take a deep breath and make my way backwards down the impossibly steep steps. The cord to the light switch hangs conveniently within arm's reach of the bottom rung.

The cellar is a small, dank space carved into the sandstone with cement foundation walls on three sides. A wooden door leads to the outside, facing the lake, but it's locked from the inside Along one wall, shelves hold cobwebbed sealers, some empty, and others whose dark contents I am reluctant to investigate. Looked like Chutney From Hell the last time I checked.

When I moved into this cottage last year, the first order of business was to replace the ancient roof, which was leaking in at least a dozen places. Aunt Ginger had an ingenious system of buckets and pans to catch the drips but the damage was done. Wood rot and stains everywhere. Fortunately for me, I was so poor I qualified for a roofing grant. Then Hope, bless her, gave up her exotic Caribbean holiday to come and help me redo the wallpaper and paint after a hardware store shopping spree.

"You're looking at your Christmas *and* birthday presents, kid sister," she'd said, stuffing the receipts into an envelope and flashing her gold caps at me. She looks a bit like Jane Fonda—definitely takes after Mother's lean, leggy family genes.

Aunt Ginger had divided her BC Telephone stocks, her Canada Savings Bonds, and her collection of foreign coins among my three siblings. These items turned out to be far more cashable, of course, than this dilapidated cottage and the land I couldn't, and wouldn't, sell. Justice still grouses about my inheriting this place, calling me landed gentry and such, but he's never lifted a finger around here, before or after Aunt Ginger died. I guess she figured that Faith and Thomas had their own law firm, Hope ran a chain of fitness spas, and Justice was a part-owner of a used car dealership, while I, the budding writer of the family, had been budding for more than a decade. Aunt Ginger correctly surmised the odds were slim I'd ever own my own home.

Our parents hadn't been able to save much after attempting to put us all through various institutions of higher learning. They'd sold their apple orchard and strawberry, raspberry, and black currant operation during the second-to-last recession and moved to a little trailer court to retire. The first holiday they took together in thirty years? Bang. A fly-by-night plane outfit travelling from Los Angeles to Mexico crashed. I was seventeen. After that, I spent most of my university breaks and Christmas holidays with Aunt Ginger here at Willow Point on Kootenay Lake.

Here's the tea trunk. Brass and blue metal. Right where I left it after first exploring this musty hole last spring. None of the six trunks are locked. I suspect all the keys are lost. The tea trunk is much smaller than the others, which contain her dance costumes, sheet music, piles of 78 rpm records, books about teaching ballet, and at least one hundred pairs of shoes. She couldn't bear to throw away shoes. She would have them repaired until there was nothing left to work with and even these she saved, lovingly wrapping each pair in dark blue tissue paper. I am unable to toss them out either, although I may donate them to the daycare just down the road so someone can have fun with them. She'd like that, I think. Much as I love the many greens and dark purples and pale yellow leathers, the dozen gleaming black patent character shoes, and the rainbow of satin dance slippers, I can't ever wear them. My feet are size six and hers were size ten.

Aunt Ginger had bought the tea ten years ago, each pound encased in heavy tinfoil, the Sinhala lion logo and Ceylon No. 1 printed on every label. The scent that rises from the opened trunk lid is a perfumed blend of tea and something else. My nose drinks it up. Not for nothing was my childhood nickname Super Nose. In our family the nickname meant respect for my ability to sniff out the turning of milk, the taint of turkey kept too long past

Christmas, the secret stash of chocolate chip cookies. But this this is a treat and I take in another big snort with gusto. I pick up a silver package from the top left-hand corner and start to close the heavy tin-lined lid.

The green marbled cover of a book peeks out where the pound of tea used to be. I put the tea on a big steamer trunk beside me and pull the book out from underneath the snugly packed double layer of tea packages. Beneath the gleaming packages are still more books with marbled-green cloth covers, each wrapped with a green silk ribbon tied neatly in a bow. Right away, I know what they are because there were two just like these upstairs in the rolltop desk.

Aunt Ginger's will had been a straightforward legal document except for her passions. We could all imagine the expressions on the notary public's face as Ginger's sequined dance dresses, Spode china, antique roses, and wooden Walton rowboats had pride of place among all the other material possessions and henceforths and thereafters:

> Please don't publish my journals or donate any of my dance costumes or music to anyone. The dresses will end up on some terrible mannequin in a museum and I'll look ridiculous by association and be completely unable to do anything about it. I trust your good judgment and hope that the family children will play dress-up with them or perhaps another dancer in the family will make good use of them. I had every intention of writing my biography of course but I couldn't stop living long enough to do that! If the writer in our family, our own Mercy Brown, can ever sit still long enough to read the journals, she may be moved to write a little article and sell it to one of the dance or women's magazines. I think the modern feminists may be interested. I don't think the lipstick-and-face-cream type of magazine would be interested unless you put a lot of sex into it. I'd rather you didn't.

Again, I trust your good judgment on this score. I realize it may not pay very well.

I had found the two green diaries in the rolltop desk, skimmed through them and, truth be told, what I found there saddened me. She had started making attempts to sum up her life but the paragraphs would trail off, the writing shaky and barely legible. One had started out being the 1981 World Jaunt journal and here, the descriptions of India, Nepal, and Sri Lanka were delightful. Aunt Ginger always loved meeting people and they, in turn, responded to her sincerity and *joie de vivre.* She never went on organized tours, preferring to make up her own itinerary. She ended up in kitchens of cooks she'd met in the marketplace, in the library of an ambassador, or on a collective onion-and-chili-pepper farm worked by formerly unemployed university graduates.

She had a major stroke in Sri Lanka as she waited to board the Air Lanka plane to Madras. When she was flown back to Canada, she, and we, discovered that she'd had several little strokes already. We also discovered, to her great embarrassment, that she'd knocked ten years off her actual birth date somewhere along the way.

The writing in the diary changed after the stroke, from the lively descriptive travelogue (and dozens of addresses) to stilted attempts to sum up her own life. Over and over she started with where she was born (Montreal) and her first dance teachers (Mlle Langlois, Mlle St. Amande) and then she tried to say what called her to dance as a vocation. "I simply *knew* I was to devote my life to the dance...I made the decision to devote my life to the art which beckoned me—the Dance...I realized at an early age, that I was, despite my proper Westmount upbringing and gangly physique, a dancer." And so on. Then her writing dissolved into illegibility, her transparent thought processes collided and crumbled, and the journal entry for that day trailed away into scribbled notes crammed along the margins, some with circles drawn around them. "Must mention Morocco...Ruth St. Denis in Santa Barbara...More on Isadora in Paris...More original Canadian works please!...Vancouver in 40s?" She tried several times, to tackle an overall outline. My Early Life. The Decision to Dance. Twenty Years of Performance. Choreography and The Duncan School of Dance. The Cottage Life. My Travels in Later Years.

I open the journal I've just found. The first page is dated October 30, 1929. Winnipeg. Her navy blue writing is ornate and confident. Youthful. Then I hear the clomp-clomp of many pairs of feet coming up the stairs to the kitchen door above me.

The Rosemont Painters. Oh no! I drop the diary back into the chest, pick up the package of tea, and scramble up the steps, banging my elbow funny bone at the very top as I lurch out. I toss the package of tea at the kitchen counter and run into the bedroom. This is what happens when you live alone and ponder every possible thing. Time goes bye-bye.

I hear a subdued group murmur, punctuated with tinkly giggles before the first tentative knock on the door.

"Be there in a minute!" I holler, trying for a spritely sort of yell instead of a desperate bid for more time. I look in the dresser mirror and see a very dark clump of cobweb with the desiccated remains of some insect life on top of my head. I pick it off and throw it in the general direction of the wastebasket beside the dresser. My hands are filthy. I yank off my jeans and T-shirt and shimmy into the pretty dress. I run on tiptoe to the bathroom and scrub my offending hands. Two violent scratches with the hairbrush and my coiffure is presentable. Jump into my sandals. Run down the hall. Stop to heave the trap door back over the gaping cellar hole. I hear an ominous crackle from somewhere between my shoulder blades. Too late to check.

"Well, hello everyone!" I trill breathlessly. (I will inspect the dress after I shepherd them all down to the lawn.) They beam at me, a sea of glinting glasses and gleaming teeth. All grasp folding lawn chairs and easels and painting supplies.

"Shall we go down to the lawns?" I suggest and shoo them down the stairs again. "Be with you in a minute! Make yourselves at home." I stop at the first turn and then, ever so casually, back slowly up the stairs. It seems I have a rip along the line of stitching keeping the zipper in place. It is only a couple of centimetres long but it troubles me. The fabric of this beautiful dress is forty or so years old and was never meant to be worn by someone heaving and hauling heavy trap doors. Still, it is barely noticeable. I'll take a chance wearing it. As long as I stick to pouring tea and holding a tray of featherweight macaroons, I'll be okay.

In less than three hours, I intend to sit down with thin white gloves on my hands, the better to handle fifty-year-old journal pages from my own personal archives downstairs in that tea trunk. In the meantime, I'll be a gracious, if somewhat distracted, host.

seven

OCTOBER 30, 1929. WINNIPEG

The Bailey Dance Company has collapsed and we girls are expected to pay the hotel bill here! Which of course we can't do because Bailey got our performance payment in advance by some means. Oh, he's a tricky one! There is no way we can afford to stay anywhere in Regina either. We are booked to dance there in four days' time. At least we all have our train tickets. We are waiting for Margery to come back from sending a telegram to the theatre people in Regina. She has a business head on her shoulders and is after them for room and board as part of our fee.

What if Bailey back in Montreal has grabbed that money as well as the Winnipeg money? How can we pay our hotel bill here when we've run up a week's worth of residence? I've proposed that one of us should distract the clerk while the rest of us file quietly out the back door with a cab waiting so we could race for the westbound train! Wouldn't that be exciting! Margery was very much against it but Chloe, Brigitte and Ida are all for it. It may be our only hope. We'll just stay at a different hotel when next we come to Winnipeg or we'll pay them back after we get to the

West Coast and make our fortune at the Orpheum. Surely this silly stock market business isn't as bad as it seems in the papers? I certainly don't see businessmen jumping out of windows in Winnipeg. They're much too sensible for that here.

OCTOBER 31, 1929

We woke up to a foot of snow this morning but the sun is melting much of it now. Margery received word back from Regina that Bailey had not cancelled our performance but had tried to get our fees ahead of time there. The Regina theatre refused to co-operate with his shady tactics, fortunately for us. Margery proposed the same fee minus room and board at the establishment they customarily dealt with and they went for this offer. What a bright girl she is! We're all very proud of her and very grateful too. As well, Ida hocked her ruby earrings and necklace set. She smiled mysteriously and said there were plenty more where that came from. Little scamp! We think there is a certain wealthy individual who admires our little Ida back in Montreal. We paid the hotel bill, thanks to Ida, and joined in the Hallowe'en party downstairs until 4 a.m. Then we packed our things and went to the Winnipeg Train Station to board the 6 a.m. train.

Snow is falling again and the whole world is white. I would like very much to practise my new piece, *La Chanson de L'Hiver pour Jonquiere* when we arrive in Regina. I would also like a chance to look at the backdrops in their theatre just in case a winter scene is appropriate. Of course, I want luxurious swaths of white cloth covered with silver sparkles and the five of us dressed in Snow Princess furs! Make believe, make believe, my favourite thing in the world to do!

NOVEMBER 1, 1929

We slept past the first breakfast call to recuperate from the shenanigans in Winnipeg. How I do love trains! We keep to ourselves to avoid the dreadful attempts at engaging our conversation by cigar-smoking men in shiny suits (one hesitates to call them gentlemen). The travelling families often eye us as though we might snatch away their children or as if they think we are some sort of travelling freak show. There are no other single women travelling on this train except us. From Toronto to Winnipeg there were a number of schoolteachers travelling together because they were to start teaching posts in smaller country places in Manitoba. Apparently they were replacing teachers who had resigned after just two months on the prairie. The Winnipeg Normal School couldn't keep up with the demand. I wonder how they are doing now with this fierce winter weather. Some of them are only seventeen years of age. I was very stung when one of the older ones told the two girls I'd been chatting with in the dining car that they were not to talk to "those dance hall girls." I have as much education and am every bit as refined as they, I'll wager. I'm certainly better travelled than that creature from Guelph in charge of them all.

NOVEMBER 2, 1929

We are comfortably ensconced in a boarding house one block from the theatre. All the theatre people stay here and the proprietor, Mrs. Digby, is not only a generous cook but an understanding soul. She has no problem with our schedule of practise and performance and keeps dinner warm for us so that we can eat afterward. Some places insist we eat at 6 p.m. or not at all, so we go without rather than dance on full stomachs.

Regina has some grand hotels and very fine homes. Chloe and Brigitte and I went out for a walk this afternoon after we had settled in at Mrs. Digby's. We were going to cross town to the legislature but the wind came up bitterly cold and we decided against that plan for today. We went to the theatre at 4 p.m. to practise for two hours. I assessed the props, Margery conducted more discussion with the Manager, who seems very sympathetic to our situation. The other girls ironed and hung costumes in the dressing room. Practise was marvellous. Everyone was very willing. The Manager appeared with tea and coffee and shortbread for us. The blizzard howled outside all the while but he reassured us that there would be an audience for tonight at 8. Indeed there was! A full house. We were introduced as the Prima Ballerinas of Mount Royal. Margery had our name changed from Bailey's Ballerinas of Mount Royal. We had a standing ovation! (We did not attempt my *Chanson* and it is the only sour note for me as it is always the piece left till the last at practise. I have a certain apprehension as to why this might be but I do not wish to create ill feelings during these trying times.)

After, we linked arms and walked in fresh falling snow back to Mrs. Digby's where we tucked into roast chicken, mashed potatoes, mashed turnips, gravy and a stupendous rhubarb cobbler. We utterly demolished the table and Mrs. Digby chuckled away at us. "You ballerinas tuck it away like a threshing gang," she said, rather proudly I thought!

NOVEMBER 3, 1929

Margery booked us for another night as the Manager persuaded her that the newspaper advertisements, new posters in several influential places and word of mouth would be sufficient to attract another good crowd.

Ida is not feeling well today so Brigitte and Chloe and I went for a good long walk across the town, near to the Royal Canadian Mounted Police headquarters. We had a grand time and stopped at a little café in the centre of town for hot chocolates. There was a poster advertising tonight's "show" at the theatre on the door! Margery sent still more telegrams to confirm our scheduled performances in Calgary, Banff and Vancouver. She is cleverly signing herself as M.B. Scott, Manager.

Everyone is resting now as I write. I am very pleased to have begun this practise of writing my daily thoughts and activities. I must write Mamma and thank her again for this pretty book and her kind words waiting for me in Winnipeg. "As I cannot discourage you from your destiny, my darling, I will wish you Godspeed." I have waited so long for her sincere best wishes to win out over Father's censure and scorn for "this unmarriageable beanpole of a daughter who flaunts herself to the public." Her words are a balm to his. I conduct myself with the utmost propriety precisely because the eyes of most of the public appraise a spirited dancer in a wispy white gown or tutu very favourably, but squint coldly with condemnation if one of us so much as laughs a little too joyously on a train platform.

At the 4 p.m. practise today I asked that we move *La Chanson* to the beginning of the practise. (Brigitte, Chloe and I had a frank discussion during our walk.) Margery said she had discussed our repertoire with the Manager, Frank Beacon, and they both agreed that the formal European pieces were most sought after on the Prairies. Many of the theatre's patrons are from Great Britain. I could see that none of the other girls were about to stand up for the piece. I stated, in as forthright and resolute a manner as I could muster, that one eight-minute work of original choreography with the theatre violinist playing Vivaldi's Winter piece would surely not disappoint the good citizens of Regina. Mr. Beacon said, "Who do we have here? Another Maud Allan?" He laughed a little bark of a laugh and Margery cast her eyes down and dimpled prettily. I shall never forgive her and I shall live to make him rue those nasty words.

As if I had asked to perform Salome and the *Dance of the Seven Veils!* It seems as if I am consigned, by my great height, to fluttering forever on bended knees at the back of the stage in ensemble pieces. I was so taken aback by this rudeness (and Margery's complicity) that I was rendered speechless. In truth, I am very stung by this decision and wept for a good long while in Mrs. Digby's utterly frigid outdoor toilet.

EIGHT

POOR GINGER! THE TYRANNY OF fear strikes again. How dare she think original thoughts? How dare she dance a new dance? The public cannot be trusted to understand! *Plus ça change...*

I'm sitting in the gloom of twilight, peering at her young dreams. We never discussed *her* young dreams. She mentioned from time to time that one of her dance pieces was being remounted, then she'd receive a modest royalty cheque in the mail and that was it.

She was the one who listened to *me* prattle on for hours about my dreams of travelling and writing and living a life of high adventure. Mother and Father were too busy working on the orchard or keeping the peace among the four of us to ever really sit down and listen. Report cards, school prizes, or 4-H meetings were discussed briefly if I had done well. "Don't want you to get a swelled head." Worst possible sin. While Justice bragged about how much money his restaurant/motel/Amway dealership/real estate/car lot was making, the women in our family quietly went about overachieving in a tight-lipped fashion. No grandiose stuff allowed. Even winning school prizes was somehow suspect. "Did the other kids clap much?" Inferring that the life of a potential egghead was friendless and fraught with resentment.

But Aunt Ginger went into overdrive on our behalf, holding up the certificate or the ribbon or the trophy. She'd loudly exclaim and beam away at us, slip us silver dollars and take us out for lunch at the Diamond Grill in downtown Nelson.

Bits of overheard conversations surface in my head, especially from the younger years when adults assumed we were too young to figure out what we were hearing. "She's not that sensible about money, never was...She's a bit old for flouncing around on her own but I imagine she's good with the little ones."

I'd never heard Aunt Ginger say one mean thing about Mother and Father and it pained me to know that all the loud and generous comments and gifts that she lavished on our family were demeaned like this, behind her flamboyant back. I know now that Grandfather's attitude toward her dance career and her morals had rubbed off on her own brother, though she never saw through it. My mother and father were financially strapped for nearly all their lives. They resented the fact that such a frivolous thing as a dance school earned Aunt Ginger enough to loan them money and to give us excessively generous gifts for any and every occasion.

I loved Aunt Ginger dearly for championing us and understanding my young dreams. I wish she could help me interpret these strange dream-visions I'm plagued with now. But I guess that's what Norman is for. I'm determined to hash out his methods if I can arrange to meet him up north. I should go to sleep now but I think I'll turn on the bedside lamp and spend more time with the journals of my perpetually young-at-heart aunt.

NINE

NOVEMBER 4, 1929

I have made my decision and kept it to myself as the other girls are too young and easily influenced, except for Margery. We boarded the train for Calgary this afternoon. We are scheduled for three evening performances there and one Saturday afternoon as well. Now Ida is definitely unwell although she recovers enough to practise and perform with seemingly no ill effects.

We are travelling Third Class coach now, having exchanged our private berth tickets in Regina so we would have the much-needed extra money for cab fares and meals. The wonderful Mrs. Digby prepared us a magnificent picnic basket, which will take us all the way to Calgary, if we don't all eat like horses. Poor Ida is not doing well with the hard uncomfortable seats and the stomach ailment, which does not allow her to benefit from the nourishment of breakfast. Chloe is tending to her very solicitously and we have attempted to fashion a bed and pillow with our coats for her so that she can curl up and possibly sleep. The train is very cold. My feet are like blocks of ice.

NOVEMBER 5, 1929

Our lodgings in the Palliser Hotel are very comfortable and it is especially nice to have an indoor water closet and a magnificent tub bath on our floor. We girls are the only residents on the fourth floor and so it is very pleasant to pass by in the hallway, to and from the bath or from visiting in our rooms. Ida and Chloe share one room and Brigitte and I and Margery occupy a rather grand corner suite with two large beds, a davenport, a little writing table and a splendid window on the main intersection of the town. Brigitte and I quickly claimed one bed for ourselves. Relations between Margery and me are very strained. I cannot meet her eye for fear of breaking into tears or worse, dramatic recriminations. I will contain myself until we get to Vancouver. It is a hard thing to admire another's talent, for she is a devoted and most delicate dancer, and has handled our business affairs so competently since the Bailey debacle, and yet also resent such a saint. Money matters seem more important than artistic programs. It seems it is ever thus in this business. I can't imagine what people will say when they hear of our little independent troupe dancing across the Great Canadian Prairies, over the Rockies and onto the balmy stages of Vancouver! So I have very divided feelings of great admiration for Margery, *esprit de corps* for our troupe and also of personal humiliation and dissatisfaction with the present and future employment of my artistic yearnings. I confess I am dreaming of many other possibilities once we arrive in Vancouver.

NOVEMBER 8, 1929

Three days have passed in a flurry of activity. We have been escorted out every evening after our sold-out performances by the Mayor, his Councillors, a Mr. Wallace and his two grown sons, William and Edgar, who are owners of a vast ranch, and

Mr. Dawson, owner of a prosperous shopping emporium here in Calgary. We have consumed enough roast beef, beefsteak and prime rib to keep our blood bright red for many months. Still more invitations were received for luncheon and afternoon tea engagements with Calgary gentlemen. We all agreed that we must not go out alone with any gentlemen and that we must all stick together unless we are ill, of course, when we make offstage public appearances. The gentlemen of Calgary have been exceedingly hospitable and I am quite sure we would all be married off in a month if we were so inclined. Mr. Wallace is a fine-looking man, a widower for twenty years, and is taller than I am, which is a small thing if one is a small woman and needn't worry about towering over a potential matrimonial candidate. Brigitte said she would marry Edgar and Chloe would go for William and they would call me Mother!! Those scamps!

Now we proceed on a brilliant winter's day to Banff. I can no longer write. The mountains approach and the girls, as well as the other passengers, many of them wealthy Americans and Europeans bound for Banff, a cosmopolitan crowd, are all clustered at the windows, exclaiming at the beauty of the landscape as we race toward these towering, ice-capped pinnacles.

NOVEMBER 10, 1929

Surely we are the luckiest girls alive to be staying in the Banff Springs Hotel! We have just the one performance, this evening, before we board the train again for Vancouver. We went for a horse-drawn sleigh ride at 2 p.m. complete with hot bricks wrapped in sacking for our feet and heavy buffalo robes to keep us bundled up and warm. We have exclaimed over the mountains, especially the peaks of Rundle and Norquay until we are left without words and yet any attempt to describe them is woefully inadequate. This is the grandest offering of Nature I have ever seen. The temperature is minus 15 but the sun is brilliant and the mountain air is so refreshing. It is cold but pleasantly so, not the same minus 15 as Montreal with the Eastern sleet storms and bone-chilling dampness. The meals here are served in grand European fashion, course after course, then we proceed to sitting rooms before roaring fires to converse over coffees before retiring. I believe I could stay here forever!

I went to practise at 3:30 p.m. and worked out my solo again, keeping Vivaldi in my head throughout, and I practically flew over the perfect floor. As I sank into the "snow" to make the grande finale angel, I looked up through the high windows circling the room and saw thick snowflakes falling ever so softly outside. Then I heard a soft clapping and "Brava, mademoiselle, brava," also very softly. When I turned my head to see who the man was, for it was a man's voice, I could see no one and with the balconies above, I could not say for certain from whence the voice came. Nonetheless, I felt a sudden pleasure that this dance, this forbidden dance, was appreciated. At this moment, however, the rest of the girls arrived, for it was 4 p.m. and time to practise ensemble pieces.

During our performance later, I saw, from my vantage point at the centre and back of the set, that several people were dozing off as we proceeded through our repertoire of selections from *Les Sylphides, Giselle* and *Swan Lake.* During the intermission, I called everyone together and again posed the question of doing my new piece. This was no strait-laced audience, I stated, and indeed, we had all met many of the assembled and agreed as to the cosmopolitan, worldly character of many of the guests. Ida, Brigitte and Chloe all murmured agreement and Margery nodded silently but kept a grim face. I bravely forged on and stated that my piece was ready and I had taken the liberty of leaving the Vivaldi music with the violinist in any case. I wished to do *La Chanson* and felt I would not disgrace any of us when I did. No one said a word. Margery nodded briefly and shrugged as she turned away. Little smiles appeared on several other faces. Then we received the five-minute call before the commencement of the second half of the programme.

I motioned the Hotel's young man over and asked him to convey my message regarding the Vivaldi piece to the violinist. We all agreed that I should dance first so that the last, long *Swan Lake* ensemble piece would end the program as usual. I took my shoes off and went out and danced as if this was to be my first and last dance. I could not watch for yawns; in fact, I was afraid to look at the audience. (Usually I am posed at the centre and back of the stage, with my arms waving like fern fronds. While the petite ballerinas enact the scenes at the centre and front of the stage, I have many opportunities to study the audience.)

When my "angel" finally descended from Heaven, bringing snow, and then remained as the Snow Angel on Earth, there was a moment of utter stillness. Then the audience clapped and clapped, roaring approval and I thought I should die with pleasure. I had made my first original dance as a professional dancer and the audience had loved it. After, everyone, even Margery, gave me great hugs and we felt the *esprit de corps* we had when we began the tour in Montreal. Our world then was very gay indeed, just one short month ago, with Bailey himself seeing us onto the train, happily attending to our great trunks of costumes.

NOVEMBER 11, 1929

Our world outside these towering fairy tale castle walls, in the snow and the mountains, is all so very splendid but there is something very much amiss with worldly economic matters. I read yesterday's *Calgary Herald* and, it seems unbelievable, but many countries, including America and Canada, will have tens of thousands of men out of work. People's investments are worthless, apparently. Many have lost their life savings. Worse news for the western provinces, the abundant grain harvest may rot for want of buyers. The suicides in the financial districts of the cities continue unabated and it is not impossible to understand now. Still and all, I think of the families of these men and I cannot agree they are better off since their fathers leapt to their deaths. I cannot imagine a mother leaping to *her* death because blue-chip stock proved otherwise. How on earth would any of this be explained to the poor orphaned children? So very sad. I must rebuff these morbid thoughts.

We boarded the train and left this enchanting place and now, as I write, we are climbing toward the Kicking Horse Pass summit, where we shall pass through a wondrous spiral tunnel, which leaves us in darkness for ages. A gentleman from Banff explained the engineering aspects beforehand so that my vivid imagination supplied the sensation of slowly spinning up and through the heart of the great mountain. It frightens Ida though and Chloe is comforting her, poor thing. Ida still feels wretched every morning. She is losing weight rapidly and has very little left on her petite frame. She has dark circles under her eyes and looks quite miserable. There was enough time to seek out a doctor from the Banff Springs Hotel or the village itself but Ida was very reluctant and timid about it as she has never before seen a doctor. Nevertheless we must all escort her to one, if need be, in Vancouver. It is obvious that she is uncommonly ill and that it is more than a temporary malady.

NOVEMBER 12, 1929

Ida has thrown herself under the train. I cannot imagine what possessed her. We are all in a state of numbed sorrow and grief for she was, until this illness, such a sunny, saucy little girl, only just twenty, not a wisp of morbidity about her. The train crew retrieved the body from the track (Margery, brave soul, identified the remains) and fashioned a temporary box until we get to Vancouver and can make arrangements. Chloe is sedated with some grains of medicine gotten from a doctor in Kamloops. Margery has begged for an empty berth for Chloe and the conductor has obliged since it is not booked for the duration of the ride to Vancouver. Altogether, the crew has been most solicitous and understanding. The man in the caboose had been looking back and saw her there on the track. Otherwise we might have gone on for many miles not knowing...I feel an odd sensation of numbness in my limbs and hollowness at my very core. I feel that I cannot feel. It is very distressing. I cannot bear to think of it and yet it is all I can think of. Oh, Ida, you sad little butterfly!

Ten

I CLOSE THE DIARY AND shake my head free of the image of white bloomers and stockings, one small black shoe still on, the shredded dress (navy blue wool, perhaps, with a dropped waistline and white Peter Pan detachable collar?), and bright patches of blood staining the snow on the track. A bloodied rag doll. The rest of them might never know that Ida was almost certainly pregnant if an autopsy was not conducted. And why should it be? Would the wealthy admirer in Montreal ever know the consequences of his dalliance? Perhaps, and it wouldn't surprise me one iota, he was married? How will the authorities, the railroad men, the police, the Kamloops coroner, describe her death? "Death by misadventure" or "A fatal accident when the young lady failed to negotiate her footing between cars" or, if the handling of the matter was not conducted with the utmost deftness by the formidable Margery, "Suicide." What cemetery would accept her body then, in 1929? What minister of any church would give final blessings?

There are at least thirty diaries in this tea chest. It's very strange that Aunt Ginger didn't identify her hiding place for them. I don't know why there was, in her mind, a need for secrecy when she openly referred to diaries in her will. I do remember thinking that perhaps they were in a safety deposit box somewhere and the key was missing. Then I reconciled myself to the possibility that there were only the two journals from the rolltop desk in her bedroom after all.

I am bowled over by what I'm reading. This is great early Canadian touring dance history, real life tragedy, the start of the Great Depression, all of it. It is impossible for me to leave them behind while I'm on my trip north. I should. I should read local histories and tourist books and maps and interview people along the Alaska Highway every waking minute. But no. I will pack these along and ration them, ten pages a night perhaps. While I ride the ferries up the coast, I'll just stretch out in the van and read, keeping Sadie Brown company as well. No dogs allowed on deck. Will she use kitty litter during the eighteen-hour boat ride between Port Hardy and Prince Rupert? Can a ten-year-old dog be retrained overnight?

Aunt Ginger is right though. Her story would make a terrific article or two or three, depending on what else I can dig up. I must search the trunk filled with her scrapbooks and old performance notices and souvenirs. It would be possible, since she was such a packrat, to piece together her itinerary with graphics as well as excerpts from her diaries. I wonder if she ever wrote anything about her childhood years anywhere? No, she mentions her mother sending her the first blank diary, so she started the habit in Winnipeg. October 30, 1929. Yes. Well, she certainly took to it. It's like hearing her talk in my ear.

Nine o'clock. The van is packed except for the diaries. Security worries niggle away at me. It is ludicrous to think of copying them all. I want to be well on my way by 7 a.m. tomorrow. If I am to catch the *Queen of Hartley Bay* ferry from Port Hardy to Prince Rupert in time to meet the *Taku* bound from Rupert to Haines, Alaska, I can't afford to spend hours meticulously photocopying thirty fragile books. Maybe I'll have the opportunity to do that somewhere en route, in Fairbanks, say, or Whitehorse. It really would be sensible. Anytime I have (a) mailed my only copy of a commissioned social studies textbook chapter done on a manual typewriter (b) lent out my most precious hardcover first edition of *Surfacing* (c) packed my slides depicting seventeen months of travelling in Europe in a cardboard box and left it with the friend of a friend (d) let Hope borrow my best dancing dress for just one special occasion...poof. Gone.

What a day. A treasure of diaries, a gaggle of painters, six left-over macaroons, a sink full of antique teacups and saucers to wash, and one skunky dog. Time to go to bed. I'll do the dishes in the morning, with a huge mug of coffee steaming on the windowsill.

I hear S.B. scratching at the door to the deck so I walk out, grabbing my old poncho and wrapping it around myself. She whirls in a tight circle and herds me to the end of the deck. She is always thrilled when I join her, anywhere, anytime. Perhaps that's why I left one husband and another left me. The joys of mutual companionship, the comfort of hearing someone else just breathing, the enduring nature of a friendship through thick and thin, are all good things cherished and maintained by a loyal dog. And are so quickly discarded by foolish and fickle women and men.

In the midst of all this excitement and packing and fifteen painters fixated on rhododendrons, I have not taken the time to take my leave of this place. I will miss this big stretch of lake and the familiar mountain across the other side. It resembles a giantess stretched out on her side, head pillowed under one arm, looking into the water, with the other long forested arm trailing into the lake. Northward, one voluptuous cedar-clothed hip rises and then slopes downward, a flashing beacon at the Narrows about where her navel would be. Right on cue, a loon calls out for Love Lost, Love Betrayed, or whatever it is that gives loons that most mournful voice, right up there with wolves in the wild and lonesome category.

Aunt Ginger. I've kept a fixed image of her as being old and kooky and lovable for as long as I'd known her. I'm twelve years older now than the Ginger I was reading this evening, dancing off into some long-gone sunset. A spinster dance teacher. Ugh what a spidery word for hard-working single women! Like Ginger Like me.

Should I have put up with philandering, disease-carrying, boozy liars for the sake of a Mrs. on my Christmas cards? Hah! Does that make me old and kooky and unlovable?

Ginger Brown. Never, ever Georgette Lucinda Brown. She ran a dance school on Vancouver Island for thirty years or more. The sad part, the big hole in my life, is that she isn't here to talk to about any of this. When she was here, I was too preoccupied with my own young self-centred life to be curious about *her* youth. She always seemed more anxious to hear all about my classes, my assignments, my opinions. She encouraged me to give her wicked descriptions of my professors and to discuss five different angles I might take with a story on spawning salmon. "Do they mate for life like some other beasties? Is there a secret inner life of the coho? I just want to be kept up to date," she'd say, patting her bright black hair and beaming at me.

A fingernail moon rises over the shoulders of the giantess across the water. I am suddenly very sad and yet so tired that I don't have the energy to have a good weep and get the emotional build-up out of my system. It's not a painful hard lump in the chest, which won't dissolve unless I howl for twelve hours. It's an unforgiving blank ache and the feeling of being somehow at fault, of being too dense to see the beauty and wisdom of someone until that someone is gone. Then, finally, much too late, I begin to grasp that there was so much more of them–Ginger, Mother, Father–to know and love. We all ran out of time. No second chances. Finito.

My heart's memory has to be content, somehow, for something like a photo of them all, with blurred grey tones, an image of them waving from inside an older model car pulling away too quickly from the camera, when what I want is a technicolour home video

I can watch a hundred times. Hit the pause button, rewind and freeze, frame by frame. All the characters and dialogue and details could be so familiar, so precise and reassuring.

ELeven

SADIE BROWN SITS IN THE passenger seat, one paw up on the armrest, long pink tongue lolling out of a hugely delighted mouth. The other paw is clasped by my right hand, my left is on the steering wheel, and with Emmylou Harris, Dolly Parton, and Linda Ronstadt warbling in three-part harmony from the tape deck, we are officially On The Road.

The diaries rest inside the tea chest on the floor between us. On top of the chest is my stainless steel thermos. My mug of coffee is anchored to the dash. This morning's cream cheese and cuke on Rudy's Bakery onion-rye bread sends a tasty combination of odours wafting through the air. My nose is happy. My dog is happy. I am happy. The Volkswagen purrs along, as well it might after sucking up $829.09. I'd be purring along too, if I were sent to a spa and coddled and steamed and wrapped with herbs and massaged by huge, gentle Swedes and fed organic fruit salads. I love driving long distances. I can understand truckers, though I hope never to look like 80 percent of them—fried cholesterol breakfasts take their toll on the human physique. I love the detachment from the telephone, from the daily routines, from any obligation except to get to some destination safely.

On my first cross-Canada drive by myself I would get lost on country roads, well off the Trans-Canada Highway, on purpose. Gas did not cost as much then. I would drive off into the unknown and end up in a fishing camp, on top of a mountain, at an abandoned homestead, or in someone's backyard. A cheery wave and a shrug and off I'd tear. I found conventional campsites aesthetically dull and sometimes frightening. I didn't have Sadie Brown then.

There was a tall, pale man in a campsite laundry room somewhere in Alberta that first trip. "So where you travelling?" "East." "So what you driving?" "A van." "So where you parked?" "*We* are just around the corner." Then he left the room. I packed up and went out to the water pump. There he was at the water pump, humming tunelessly and staring at me. I pretended not to recognize him. I walked back to my van, started it up and left that perfectly nice campground in a cloud of dust, forfeiting my overnight fee. Nowadays, I'd go straight to the campground attendant and insist on an identity check for the guy at the nearest RCMP. A sicko on the prowl won't stop just because one selected target got away.

On side roads and other unpaid spots, I took to putting my bush boots upon the passenger seat. If anyone nosy meandered by, they'd think a burly construction worker was stretched out in the back. It's true I kept a hammer under my pillow, but how I thought a pair of size six Kodiaks would deter sinister travellers is darkly amusing to me these days.

Now I have Sadie Brown who is so loyal that she will mash her teeth up against the windows and snarl in the most vicious way if anyone so much as walks by the vehicle. She has reliable instincts about human character and would have sent the likes of the tall, pale man packing with a menacing series of growls. She is deceptively beautiful, with a flowing golden coat, white throat and underbelly, and an intelligent border collie head. However, she is equal parts German shepherd, blue heeler, border collie, and coyote. I think I started out as her mother when she was ten weeks old and over the years the roles gradually reversed—in her head at least. She would be dangerous if anyone got close to me with evil intentions. I like that.

We barrel along through two mountain ranges on a perfectly dry highway with zilch for traffic. I believe in travelling on Tuesdays for this very reason—just the open road except for the long distance trucks and delivery vehicles.

The long descent to the bottom of a fruit-farming valley takes all my attention now. No gazing off at glaciers and peaks and high altitude lakes still trapped in green ice. The van negotiates the hairpin turns with ease. I send telepathic thanks to my excellent mechanic who spotted the worn-out front brake pads. In nine ear-popping minutes we're purring along beside a long narrow lake. Peach, cherry, apple, and plum trees grow halfway up the valley sides, flanking the lake. Blossom season is over in this dry belt. Water sprinkler systems spray away as we drive through. The sun shines on the droplets, creating hundreds of shimmering rainbows under the trees.

Time for a fill-up and a stretch for both of us. We've been driving without a break for nearly four hours. At the main intersection of Osoyoos we pull into a gas station, fill up with gas and park beside a long truck loaded with Hereford cattle. One cow presses her damp nose against the gap between the slats and blows noisily through her nostrils. Sadie Brown prances at the end of her leash, sniffing the heavy odour of at least thirty cattle all crammed together. This old cow lowers her head a little and shakes it, blowing another warning snort. S.B. must remind her of the farm dog left behind on some Rock Creek ranch.

"Poor old thing," I coo. "Didn't pump out calf number nine this spring? Is that the way it is? No retirement with dignity for you?"

She shakes her head and blows air out her nostrils. What a life. She has mournful deep brown eyes and I swim in them for a long few seconds. Sadie Brown sits close to me, a little fearful, peering up through her failing eyes at the cow.

Something is niggling at me as I turn and begin a brisk walk down a road between two orchards. Did I leave the kettle on the stove? No, it's in the van with the rest of the kitchen camping stuff. The house then? Did I forget to leave a key for Corey? No, of course I did. I transacted the post office business. Everything. I've checked off my list and there isn't a thing left undone that really had to be done. Really, I worry too much sometimes.

When we get back to the van, the big cattle truck is gone, leaving only a faint trace of acrid scent hanging in the air. There it is again. The niggling feeling. The smell of fear. I think I can call it up if I close my eyes and rely on my nose. Yes. My friend Leah's farm a mile from ours. The truck full of young steers pulling out of the yard and several of the mother cows lurching behind it, bellowing pitifully, their trapped sons wailing back at them. Leah and I run to a place far back in their pasture where the old workhorse stands dozing. Leah cries and cries and so do I, both of us leaning against the big white belly of an old Percheron mare.

There are some pictures that never disappear in the mind's eye, like a slide permanently stuck in the projector, the old brain carousel. This one of the brown and white cattle bawling and running, their udders swinging, their eyes wild, and the stock truck rumbling up the hill and away with their babies bound for the slaughterhouse will stick with me forever.

That's not all there is to this niggling pressure. I think I'm starting to recognize the advance guard of one of these seismic visions of mine. They stem from my Super Nose. An evocative scent will give me the initial sensory recognition and then a host of past associations swirl in. Occasionally, something will move beyond the established sensory membrane, beyond pleasure like lilacs or searing nostalgia, like a decomposing animal carcass. Last time, on the deck of the cottage, it may have been the new spring smell of lake water rising with spring run-off that propelled me into the vision of the flooding river. It's as if there is a deep well of intuition, which reflects something clearly, a tiny brown face my own face, peering into the mystery of itself.

Sadie Brown butts her head against my leg. Time to get going by her clock, I guess. Poor old dear is so patient with my habit of stopping all earthly progress and floating away on dream time.

On the road again, with Doug and the Slugs' rhythm and blues belting out of the tape deck. We clip along past turn-of-the-century mining towns, shrunk to one main street with several tall and handsome brick buildings, gracious Victorian two-tone wood frame houses, and an astonishing number and variety of churches. Century-old smokestacks stand like sentinels and in one narrow valley, the gap-toothed wooden remains of mineshafts cling to the sides of the mountains. Abandoned pink brick communal Doukhobor houses, trailer courts, three-bedroom bungalows with manicured lawns in the middle of nowhere, closed fruit stands, fields full of cattle with bright new calves, and horses with lanky little foals blur by. More mountains, waterfalls, rivers, trees. I put in my tape of Vivaldi's *Four Seasons* with that crackerjack British violinist Nigel Kennedy to complement the semi-desert stretches, the calves and foals, the running water, the snow peaks. Aunt Ginger would have loved Nigel Kennedy's way with Vivaldi.

The highway plummets through the last misty mountain pass into the Fraser Valley. Here are the greenest green fields, prosperous dairy farms, the unmistakable odour of swine in large numbers, posh riding stables, spreading subdivisions and condominiums on the valley sides, hulking like angular pastel warts on the horizon above the farmlands.

Perfect timing. The afternoon rush hour is over and we zip through the city of Vancouver, over the Lions Gate Bridge and finally, down to the Horseshoe Bay ferry terminal. I see, with a sinking feeling, a large ferry backing away from the dock. The fee collector confirms my suspicions. We have almost an hour to wait for the next ferry. This is not the end of the world.

Again, it is high time that Sadie Brown and I stretched our legs.

I climb down, feeling the stodgy sort of stiffness that only sitting for five hours straight can entrench in the human body. S.B. stretches out both of her hind legs, one at a time, and then prances away from the leash. She is a permanent teenager at heart no matter that her pancreas has stopped functioning and her eyes are clouded with the first blue film of cataracts. I reach back inside to shut the van lights off and lock up. Then we set out at a fast clip, looking for a discreet patch of earth for her necessary functions. Acres of asphalt are hard on a dog. We make our way to a scrubby shoulder of ground at the far end of the parking lot, crowded by prickly blackberry bushes. S.B. relieves herself and I unkink my shoulder, neck, and arm muscles. We walk along the side of the lot for several more minutes but it seems the petrochemical fumes have dulled her usual pleasure in sniffing out new and smelly substances.

Back at the van, I succumb to the urge for a short power nap on the back seat. Sadie laps at her water and then stretches out again with a contented sigh. I'll hear the blast of the ferry horn as it comes into the cove. It's been a long day, starting at 5:30, and my eyes feel so much better closed like this.

TWELVE

Inside the Vegetable Shed, she is standing beside Dai Thomas, judging vegetables. It's a very large exhibit and it's hot. They've been at it since 7:30 that morning.

"Let's finish up this lot and have an orange-ade break," wheezes Dai.

"I couldn't agree more," the new judge responds gratefully. Dai Thomas is the Senior Judge and she was asked to be his assistant for the first time this year.

"Peas! Bloody peas! Carrots, spuds, beets, and turnips I can single out in a minute. But peas!" he fumes, tapping his clipboard none too gently with his pencil.

"Let's see," she says, briskly. "Uniform size, not over blown, no scars, open up a pod for size. Proper showing." Her hands shell one pea pod per plate as she lists the judging criteria.

"Look here! Under-size, over-size, and white fungus! Here we go, three decent specimens. Let's count peas to the pod. Seven, six, eight! Taste finally...all good, really. So let's give it to our top producer here. Hah! Four minutes flat. Ribbons please, sir!"

"Good work, lass. Now let's pop over to the concession stand and get something to sustain us through the ruddy useless marrows and pumpkins, shall we?"

Despite the thirty-degree heat, Dai Thomas wears a tweed suit coat and matching vest and pants. At the start of the day he wore a brown pork-pie hat on his mop of grey hair. He abandoned it midway through the red and green cabbages.

"And how are you making out, both of you?" asks the little sparrow of a woman in the Women's Institute concession booth as she hands them their drinks.

"Good showing, despite the drought," says Dai, after a healthy swig. "Would you mind topping that up for me? Thirsty work, this."

"Oh certainly, Mr. Thomas," she flutters. Her daughter's coddled vegetable marrow is on show in all its pale-skinned glory, started in February with a special light bulb in the house, of all things.

"Thank you kindly, Mrs. Morrow," says Dai, reaching up for his hat brim to tug, but ending up making a little salute instead. The two judges return to the Vegetable Shed, refreshed and ready to do battle with the finer points of vegetable showmanship: true to type, ripeness, absence of mechanical, bacterial, or viral damage, and the interior evidence of regular watering, hilling and soil preparation.

"You'll be pleased to see there are only four marrows on exhibit," the new judge says. "Two unfit for showing. What a waste to pick them so small. This thing is huge. This one is fair to middling. What to do?"

"The ribbons, Madam. Although we might want to withhold a first place in this sorry lot except for this monstrous one. Bloody shame they were invented in the first place. Who eats them, I ask you?"

"Some people stuff them with bread and raisins, I hear."

"Agghh! Bloody horrible!"

They proceed to the major garden exhibits that take pride of place on the long paper-covered table. Eight garden vegetables and two varieties of annual garden flowers. Some are artfully arranged in wicker baskets, cornucopia style. Some are placed on massive card-board podiums sheathed in green crepe paper. Still others are displayed in camouflaged boxes, the kind baby chicks arrive in off the plane from Edmonton hatcheries. Snapdragons, clarkia, bachelor buttons and cosmos are the hardy favourites while sweet peas fill the air with their heady fragrance. Homemade labels indicating variety—Nantes Half-Long Carrots, Homesteader Peas, Detroit Dark Red Beets, Ultra Girl Tomatoes—are strategically placed in each exhibit.

Dai Thomas has his doubts about the most magnificent display. He's eyeing the tomatoes.

"It doesn't say they're greenhouse-raised, but I'll bet my bottom dollar they are...and the label ought to say so," he pronounces after a lengthy deliberation. "We are looking at Best of Show category, after all."

She studies the problematic tomatoes. "To tell the truth, I much prefer this display here," she says, pointing to a converted baby chick box lined with oat straw. "Three varieties of potato, two each of carrot turnip, beet and late lettuce. Beautiful stuff. Lovely old-fashioned flower bouquet, perfect pickling cukes, cherry tomatoes, and three types of bean, all in prime condition. It's more representative of a family garden than this flashy effort."

She points to the huge tomatoes nestled beside English cucumbers and green peppers.

"I'm torn, I truly am," he declares. "We can't fault anyone for going all-out with a greenhouse and forcing stuff along. It's no easy feat to beat the frost in this country with the likes of these." They contemplate the hothouse beauties glumly.

"We have here," he stands up straight, "a dilemma on our hands. To reward new advances and vigilance in northern horticulture, or the steadfast virtues of a bountiful family garden, the tried and true.'

She looks for a technicality to break the deadlock. A missing label, too few or too many vegetables per plate, a concealed sunburn, perhaps a clever fingernail nicking off potato scab. Sighing, she hefts a tomato from each exhibit and looks at her confounded colleague.

"The knife please, sir."

The evidence is plain to both sets of eyes. Dai offers a magnificent blue rosette to arrange on the display with firm, vine-ripened tomatoes while the watery discharge from the hothouse experiment leaks onto the green crepe paper bedding of the more elaborate exhibit.

"A job well done," he says, saluting briskly. "Decisiveness and a solid

command of show vegetable criteria, these things the astute judge must possess," he says, tapping his clipboard for emphasis and smiling. 'Furthermore, anyone who grows three varieties of potato commands more respect than a green pepper dilettante, in my books, speaking quite confidentially to a fellow judge," he adds, offering his arm as they stroll down the aisles of prize-winning produce to retrieve the pork-pie hat back in red cabbages.

THIRTEEN

I AM LOOKING UP AT the ceiling of the van, as if through the wrong end of binoculars. A fly is droning monotonously somewhere near the front, stopping, starting, stopping again. I feel very content, swaddled here in my pillows and blankets, a steady breeze plying back and forth through the screen windows.

Then the ceiling looms nearer, descending, and I struggle to sit up, rolling over onto one elbow. There is a small sick hot spot in my upper chest, moving toward my throat. I swipe my fist along my clammy upper lip and take a couple of deep breaths until the hot spot dissolves and I feel okay again. S.B. cocks an inquiring eye at me.

"I feel...weebly, old bean," I say, clearing my throat. Thump, thump, thump. Instant sympathy. I grope around for a pen and a scribbler I have stashed back here somewhere. A big long technicolour dream. I write down the elements of it as fast as I can.

Outside, motors rev up and a wave of foul exhaust fumes floats through my air. I sit upright, realizing that this might be my ferry to catch. The lot is filled with vehicles. I scramble up to the wheel but before I get the key into the ignition, I look out and see that we're in the second to last line and the ferry attendant is holding us right where we are. Oh no, another hour to wait. I'm feeling groggy and polluted. I want to get out of this parking lot and onto the boat and into some clean air and fast!

I crawl back into the comfort of my pillows. May as well rest when I can. I shove the scribbler to one side and curl up again. S.B. snuffles in a contented way below me on the floor. No big deal. If I could just turn my nose off, I'd be all set. Outside, the ship's horn blares and then, a cool evening breeze, salty but reasonably fresh, floods through my screen windows and I drink it up gratefully.

Another ferry boat horn, from farther away, blares twice with a throaty *basso profundo* and yet another, a smaller craft closer by, emits three brassy yips. The reassuring voices of the boat community at sea. I close my tired eyes again.

FOURTEEN

It sounds like someone is trying to use the big Fair loudspeaker again, getting lots of ear-popping static and crackling feedback for their efforts. There are several horns blaring. Maybe the tractor pull has started.

The green jeeps arrive first and then the sky fills with helicopters in formation. One boy counts thirty as he hides in the loft of the red barn.

"What in blazes do we have here then?" Dai Thomas demands to know, dabbing with a napkin at a spot of mustard on his chin. They stay in the shade of the awning of the Women's Institute Supper Tent, peering out and up.

"I don't have a clue! But look at that man with the loudspeaker!" The new judge points at a tall man with a hawkish profile. She grips her paper plate filled with raspberry shortcake and stares at the speaker who is somehow familiar.

The rumble of the helicopters drowns out the man's words. He looks up angrily and reaches for a beeper into which he shouts something unintelligible. The helicopters move up and sideways like a cloud of silver and black grasshoppers. People stare after them, while the cattle bawl in the barn, several horses rear in the ring, and chickens squawk in their cages.

"Read my lips!" the man yells, looking at his right-hand man with a smirk.

"Everyone, attention!" the man bellows. Then there is silence except for the sounds of babies and animals. "This is an emergency evacuation. You are asked at this time to leave the Fairgrounds by the west gate on foot. Don't worry about the livestock. I repeat, leave by the west gate. Immediately."

Absolute silence for a split second. The phalanx of helicopters drones faintly now. Then the roar of hundreds of voices. They surge forward in a great, ragged wave. Men and women yell the names of husbands, wives, children, parents. The children are big-eyed and silent, except for the very small ones who keep asking "Why? Why?"

"Let's skedaddle, Eldon," hisses a young woman nearby as she pulls the toddler back from the main body of the crowd and keeps her right arm curved around a very new baby wrapped in a fleecy yellow blanket.

The new judge cannot believe her eyes. The 4-H pledge comes unbidden to her mind.

I pledge my head to clearer thinking

She tries, then, to think.

Telescopic rifles are raised by the men in jeeps. She counts over twenty jeeps before losing track.

The noise is deafening as the jeeps rev up and the helicopters hover directly overhead. The dark brown dust skirls everywhere, whipped up by the choppers. She thinks she hears several shots.

A child runs by, almost bumping into Dai Thomas. The lad carries a large black rabbit, which stares pinkly at the world. An elderly woman hobbles along with a jar of canned peaches and her handbag.

"Turn the animals loose!" yells a teenage girl as she dodges a jeep and runs toward the barn. Two others join her, one boy in an all-white dairy show outfit and a young woman in a semi-formal velvet dress with sling-back silver sandals. Her tiara topples off, and she kicks away her sandals to sprint on nyloned feet through the crowd.

The new judge turns to speak to Dai Thomas but he isn't beside her. She ducks back into the Supper Tent and crawls out under the opposite side. She stays low as she runs behind the outdoor toilets and heads for the parking lot.

Too late. Three jeeps guard it and the men have rifles ready. Several other fairgoers are turned back to the crowd. The jeep closest to her has a wolf tail dangling from the antenna. Phone! She has to get to a phone. There must be one in the old yellow house.

There is a small stampede of calves and sheep, but almost all of the people are beyond the main thoroughfare of the grounds. The helicopters hover over them. The new judge decides to make a dash through the cattle that are being chased out of the barn, but a jeep swerves around the corner. Five men wearing rubber pig masks and holding cellular phones sit in it, pointing at her. The driver leans on the horn continually, but two monstrous bulls, one Charolais, one Red Polled Shorthorn, amble in front of the vehicle. She uses the moment to dash into the yellow house.

A pot of tea and several cups, steam still rising from them, are abandoned at the old yellow formica table. The house is still and quiet except for a radio somewhere upstairs. An old-fashioned black telephone on the wall next to her is dead. She slams her hand on the door jamb. The faded green gingham curtains flutter as another jeep roars past. She ducks and then, staying low, she finds the stairs and makes her way up.

Then she hears a different kind of motor, a higher pitch than the jeeps. Right past the porch downstairs roars Dai Thomas with an elderly woman in a print housedress on the back of his motorcycle. A black World War II vintage Indian. Now she sees a jeep at the south entrance turn to follow them, two jeep-men standing up, aiming their rifles. She races down the stairs and through the kitchen.

"NO!" she screams, jumping off the steps of the kitchen door, landing in front of the jeep. It swerves in a spray of gravel and dust.

"Get a move on, lady," one jeep-man shouts, waving the rifle at her. She turns and runs.

She hears the jeep stall and a curse, as she zigzags into the big red barn.

I am in a violent American movie. I am even running away from men with guns. I am in shock.

The 4-H pledge phrases roll through her head again.

My heart to greater loyalty

A dapple-grey horse stands with its lead rope untied, one end on the ground in front of her. The jeep roars past the barn. She walks slowly toward the horse, murmuring, "Don't bolt, lovey, don't bolt." The horse pricks its ears up with interest but stays put until led to a wooden pen.

She climbs up the slats of the pen, trying to ignore the huge sow sniffing at her legs and the piglets squealing in the straw below. She turns awkwardly, urging the horse closer until she can get one leg slung over its back. With a push and a leap, she straddles the horse and they walk over to the open doors. She can see one jeep still circling at the eastern end of the grounds and several men patrolling the buildings, carrying their rifles, hollering back and forth. "Clean? Yo!"

She leans over the horse's neck to tie the lead rope in a single loop, trusting the horse to neck-rein as well as he was trained to stay put when ground-tied. Then she takes a deep breath and digs in her heels. The horse breaks into a startled trot and then, with another dig and a slap on the rump, he breaks into a lope as they clear the open doors.

"Oh, you sweetheart!" she whispers as he turns left again without breaking stride, responding to a mere touch of the rope. Someone shouts behind them but they are covering ground fast with the horse's rocking-chair gait. Straight ahead is a closed barbed-wire fence.

"Omigod! No!" She hauls back on the rope but there is no bit to restrain the horse. There is more shouting and the roar of a jeep. The horse keeps plunging forward and she grabs for the coarse black mane, thinking crazily of a teenage Elizabeth Taylor in National Velvet. *Without so much as a lurch, they soar over the gate and gallop down the dirt road.*

In seconds they reach another gate but this one is already open, a tangled mess of wire and poles on the ground. They slow down to a walk, picking their way around the wire.

Again they speed up to an easy lope as they come to a large hay field with alfalfa drying in swaths and the baler and tractor standing idle at the far end. She stops and listens, looking skyward. The helicopters travel in a long line more than a few kilometres away from where she is. She turns the horse to follow the edge of the field, staying close to the fringe of trees so they can head under cover at the first sound of motors coming closer. When they reach the end of the field, they enter a thinly wooded stretch of poplars.

In minutes they emerge onto high banks covered with sage and saskatoon bushes. There is no fence so she risks being out in the open to move forward to a lookout point.

"I've got to see where they're going," she says out loud. The horse perks up his ears and they move toward a smallish clump of chokecherries and young poplars, high enough to camouflage both horse and rider. She is close enough to see the long line of people and aghast to see a dirty brown tide of water lapping only ten feet from the top of the bank. A big herd of white-faced cattle is climbing up the opposite side of the valley, with the muddy water at the heels of the stragglers. She thinks she hears the theme song from that show with Lorne Greene as the Pa and Little Joe and Hoss and their big brother Adam who always wore black. Nine o'clock on Sunday night, right after Ed Sullivan. "Bonanza."

She squints and strains to see better but the Fairground people are just tiny figures. She recognizes animals by their shapes and she can also see the jeeps. Somebody is firing shots. The tiny people are walking into the water and the shots keep ringing out, even as the heads bob and the arms thrash. She sees a large white cow, or bull, drop and roll end over end down the ridge and into the water. The helicopters swerve overhead.

"The bastards! They're shooting from above!" she shrieks. The horse jumps at this outburst but calms down as he has his neck and shoulder patted. She tries to calm herself down too but this is impossible. She cannot stand to look at the ridge again or to keep listening to the piercing screams. Human or animal? She can't tell anymore.

She looks down and sees the water spilling over the bank nearest to her.

"We've got to head for the highway, my fine boyo," she says to the horse, as they cross the field at a lope. This time they jump both gates although she nearly falls off when he swerves to clear the fallen gate safely. She congratulates herself for wearing a culotte skirt and sensible walking shoes for her day of judging at the Fair. She stifles a nervous laugh, which threatens to go on and on.

My hands to larger service

They gallop through the deserted Fairgrounds and race for the entrance to the highway. They slow down to follow the old asphalt road, trotting on the dirt shoulder until they come to the first intersection. They stop at the signpost.

It's a gleaming blue and yellow sign, shaped like an unfurling flag. The dirt is freshly dug around the base of the post. An old black and white sign is face up in the ditch. She feels nausea rising and her hands and knees shake. The new sign says New Horizon, Unincorporated. That's crazy nonsense! The old sign in the ditch says what it said this morning when she drove past it at seven o'clock: Wide Sky Country Fairgrounds, 1 km.

She clucks to the horse and they move forward, staying off the asphalt. With luck, they could reach town in three hours.

Someone would tell them what happened—it would be on the news.

She would stop at the first farmhouse and use their phone but she has a feeling it won't be working and no one will be in the house anyway. She leans down and pats the horse's sweaty grey neck again.

And my health to better living

For my club, my community, and my country

The wind picks up, blowing a fine dust of topsoil into her face. The drought has been going on twenty-five days now. It'll ruin the crops. She fights back a shudder.

Nothing is right anymore. Everyone's gone and the air smells like water.

FIFTeen

I AM SHAKING, MY WHOLE body in a horizontal jitterbug. I manage to reach for the nearest cupboard handle. As I pull myself up to a sitting position I roll over and fall off the bunk. I'm suddenly wet and S.B. stands over me, whimpering and nudging at my face. I try to pull myself together, try to get back into my own body, but my body is on the floor of the van and I am soaked from the waist up.

I hear vehicles passing by. The ferry! I get myself up, shove Sadie's spilled water pail aside, and stagger up to start the van. I've spilled her water all over me *and* the floor of the van. Hell's bells! I decide to drive up to the head of my empty row and let the ferry attendant decide what to do with me. All the other vehicles are smoothly proceeding onto the *Queen of Nanaimo.*

The ferry attendant gives me a perplexed look but she waves me on, into the dark cave of the ferry. Thank you, thank you. I hang onto the steering wheel, still feeling disoriented, with my clammy dog-water sweatshirt clinging to my back, another solid thump on my head and a cotton-ball mouth. I pull in behind a Greyhound bus and park.

That was the biggest, longest, most lurid vision yet. I have to get notes done before I go anywhere, before things fade. Then I have to get them to Norman somehow. I get up and reach into my little fridge for a cold bottle of water; I have to do something about this cotton-mouth before I can collect what's left of my wits. I fish out a dog biscuit for Sadie as well. She gives me a grateful look and picks it off my flat palm with delicate restraint before crushing it with gusto. I reach past her for my blue notebook in the glove compartment.

The elements of the vision first. I scribble away under the van's overhead light, the low grumble of the ferry motor blotting out the other noises of the world. I am getting better at recalling these things that I do know. Somehow these personal symbols, these dream creations of all of us who are plugged into Norman's system are like human pheromones. He explained this bit of hormonal lore to me during the Nitassinan work.

Apparently, moths, mice, bees, and women in dormitories all release minute quantities of biological information, which cause a specific response when detected by the same or a closely related species. Sometimes this means that, in the case of bees, ovarian development by other female bees is suppressed on orders from the queen bee's hormones. In the case of women in dormitories, often after roommates live together a couple of months in close quarters, their menstrual cycles synchronize. Men in love grow beards faster than usual and people who do a lot of kissing are found to produce a lot of sebum which those in the know—the kissee and kisser—can detect subconsciously. Sexy stuff, sebum, when it's not just perceived as waxy skin oils clogging our pores. There is also evidence to suggest that trees and other plants pass along information to each other about approaching fire, disease, and predatory bugs. Norman says our human dream elements are conventionally interpreted as individual manifestations of fear, confusion, or love, a working-out of those highly personal matters, which our conscious minds can't yet comprehend, recognize, or bear to accept.

The British Premonitions Bureau was founded to receive and

analyze predictions and dreams after the disastrous slag heap slide on the Welsh mining village of Aberfan. Far too many people from all over Britain, had had nightmares and other precognitive visions prior to the catastrophe. If their foreknowledge had been co-ordinated and acted upon, over one hundred school children and adults might have been spared a dreadful death.

One little girl in Aberfan told her mother at breakfast that she'd had a dream of going to her school but there was no school there. Something black had come down all over it. The very next morning, she went to school and suffocated under half a million tonnes of coal-mining waste.

Other people woke from nightmares about bedroom walls caving in on them, about a child in a telephone booth screaming, and a black mountain moving with children buried beneath it. An elderly man in England saw letters in his dream, which did not make sense to him:

A B E R F A N.

Aberfan is the reason I do the sensory reception reports for Norman. I responded to his advertisement in *The Globe and Mail* three years ago, in the "Personals" where I still go to comfort myself that I am not yet so isolated and desperate that I need to advertise myself as terminally frisky yet intelligent and sincere. That Saturday edition had the ad that promised insight, relief or even an end to what I understood as my little "quirk":

> Computer programmer interested in Canadians who experience precognitive dreams, day or night, with verifiable outcomes. Contact Norman Joe Szabo, fax 403-633-6351. No telephone calls will be accepted.

In my response, I tried to condense what I recognized as precognitive insights into two pages. I worked for a full day on those two pages. First of all, I stressed that I was not under the influence of medicinal or recreational drugs or alcohol, that I did not invite these visions and that I would much rather do without them. I was not a follower of the occult, pagan, or New Age religions either. I had not yet worked out the details of my spiritual place in the universe, other than to trust completely in angels, a comforting, if childish, world view. Bits of all the major religions made sense to me. However, I felt it was my responsibility to contribute what I'd experienced because of Aberfan and other instances where it might be crucial to speak up despite the fear of ridicule.

Secondly, I wrote up a list of my precognitions. There was the time I knew Ollie Ringwald was dead before his car rolled down the riverbanks. And when Dawna Glassco walked into the river with her face set and pale. Also the time that a husband (mine) had not one, but two, affairs going on simultaneously. This last instance, however, could be attributed to just plain common sense; I had observed that he was happy *and* exhausted all the time yet he had no gainful employment to inspire him or to tire him out much either.

I "saw" the train wreck in the Rockies, two engines rearing up like horses, hooves flailing, cars twisting, falling, bursting into flames. Another time I was haunted by a killing blizzard on the Prairies. I "saw" stranded cars and frozen corpses inside. Truly horrific. I had no one to talk to about it and I had no peace of mind because the images would return to me, day and night. I made the mistake of spilling my guts to a friend, who gleefully announced to everyone that I had slipped my moorings.

Two days later the blizzard showed up on the news. Sure, there are killing blizzards every winter and people who defy the weather and go out in it and die. But why then, did the black and white photo in the newspaper reveal what I'd already envisioned: an elderly couple slumped together with those same coats, with his tartan scarf and her dark hand-knit hat? In their big black Oldsmobile that had slid off the road?

I'd finished up my list of precognitive insights with the time a friend's ex-wife, hoping to cause him grief and suffering, stole his dog. I immediately knew where she'd taken him, actually "saw" Rufus sitting on the edge of a pier. I phoned the ex-wife and told her the jig was up with as much authority as I could muster. Within two hours, the dog was on my doorstep. That instance could also be traced to common sense and understanding a little of jealousy and revenge. After all, if she could smuggle her latest lover out to their cottage every Thursday afternoon, why not her ex-husband's Airedale?

My most favourite recent episode involved an administrator who'd taken several files from my desk in order to prevent a somewhat scathing report I'd written from reaching the directors. "Are you sure they're missing?" she'd asked, scrutinizing me from top to toe. "I haven't seen them." And at that very instant I "saw" them in a big green metal box as I stared into her beady brown eyes. I turned and ran down five flights of stairs to the dumpster. Voilà! Under a day's worth of garbage were the very files in question. The administrator's excuses were priceless. "I must have knocked them into the garbage when I was tidying up the office...Oh, it's all my fault. I just get so carried away cleaning up." Cleaning up *my* office?

So. My visions consisted of several instances of basic treachery and others in the nightmare category created, perhaps, by too much spicy food too late at night. Some visions, however, were not accountable to any objective criteria or shrewd deduction or Cajun calories. What impelled me to contact Norman Joe Szabo were my dreams of tremendous noise, the roaring all around me, the sensation of being trapped in willows and muskeg in a place which, weeks later, we identified as Nitassinan. I'd grope my way out of these frightening visions with my heart going a million miles an hour.

With myself and at least thirty others reporting visions like this, Norman found a place inundated with low-level jet aircraft flights and constant deafening noise that drove every living thing on the ground bonkers. The political and legal problem was how to present enough information about the detrimental effects of this bombardment.

Somehow, between setting up the information network system and analyzing the dream elements, Norman was able to pinpoint many routes taken by the animals on which Innu families depended for food. The animals' migration routes, mating and calving areas, summer and winter pastures, were wide-ranging and diverse. Independent wildlife biologists monitored the rates of miscarriage, calf mortality and inability to reproduce in otherwise healthy caribou and moose, protein staples of the Innu. Norman's maps created a very different picture of so-called "desolate" land than that held up by the military, who had never lived off the land. Lawyers combined the knowledge of the Innu people's hunting areas and the amount they needed to hunt to survive with the figures from the biologists and Norman's maps. It all added up to a winning case in the Supreme Court of Canada.

I also came clean in the initial report to Norman about the times I'd never seen anything come to pass after even the most vivid dreams. Our neighbour's granaries did not explode—I'd heard about the phenomenon of spontaneous combustion on the radio and imagined well the possibilities. My parents were not amused. My science teacher did not run away with the drama teacher, as I had dreamt. He married the home economics teacher during the Christmas break. We girls thought that the drama teacher was the prettiest teacher in the whole world and the science teacher the handsomest; as they say in algebra, we thought they would make the divine equation. A well-balanced diet and child-bearing hips won out over beauty and her zippy red sports car. We'd whisper "Canada Food Rules!" whenever we wanted to send each other into giggle spasms during science labs for the rest of grade eight.

It took me a very long time after the clarity of childhood to distinguish a genuine extra-sensory insight from my own emotional agenda, which projected qualities or motives onto others. Instead of receiving clear symbols and situations as I had in my preteen years, uncomplicated by hormones, calculus or social hierarchies, I agonized as to whether my green dress was too weird to wear with running shoes. That sort of hopeless bathos did not qualify as seismic information and I was adrift for at least a decade while I focused on high school graduation and, later, a master's political geography thesis. My sense of the visions as being a vital conduit to complex truths dried up and blew away. I completely forgot about them, in fact. My head was filled with assignments and deadlines and my heart with the usual youthful hopes and fears. At least, I thought they were the usual: good grades, safely contained romances, summer jobs, nifty clothes, lots of friends to party with, getting away from the orchard to go to university in the big city.

In order to retain my credibility, I didn't confess to Norman all the wrong-headed instances when I succumbed to my own concocted visions of togetherness in the pursuit of romance. How would it sound if I spent two pages describing how I consistently confused genuinely *nice*, kind, intelligent men with the terminally dull? How I ripped my heart and liver into shreds for the dubious affections of a long string of charming cads and bounders? I would have come across as a willfully blind nitwit with a tin ear and hot-to-trot as well. This image of myself did not jibe with my own politically correct version of myself as a hard-working, fun-loving person, fiercely loyal to her friends and at ease with a large throng of pleasant acquaintances, a Good Girl at heart, if not in deed.

sixteen

THE NOXIOUS DIESEL FUMES OF the Greyhound bus jolt me into prime time and my hand automatically reaches for the ignition. We drive off the *Queen of Nanaimo* with the lights of the city glittering ahead of us. I want to drive straight out onto the highway heading north before I pull over and stop for the night. The time to splurge on motels is much further along my journey than one long day's drive from home. Or is it? That spot between my shoulder blades aches.

One sign announces Kozy Kove Kampground, 1 km. I step on the gas. People who use K's like that ought to be fined or publicly humiliated in some way. My revenge, though they may never know it since I neglect to stop and tell them, is to boycott such places on the grounds of bad taste and horrific abuse of the English language.

The next sign says Wildwood Campground, open June 1st. It is now the thirtieth of May. Onward. Sadie Brown rests her head on my knee and looks up at me, emitting a little sigh of her own. She's right. It is time we stopped this constant motion.

Fleming Campsites Ahead. Open May 1-November 1. We're in business if it isn't booked. We kathunkety-thunk down a bumpy little lane and stop in front of an old-fashioned white and green wooden cottage. It is almost nine o'clock but the lights are still on. I hop out and spring up the steps, open a screen door and enter a tiny office with a massive front counter.

A brilliant orange head of hair bobs up from behind the counter, followed by heart-shaped glasses, black-rimmed bright green eyes, a little pug nose and violently orange lips. The total effect is a merging of Mick Jagger and Lucille Ball. I smile hugely at this person.

"Yes good evening how many?" she asks, flipping open a registry book.

"One," I say, still smiling. "Just an overnight." She raises one pencilled black eyebrow.

"I see a dog what about your dog?"

"Oh yes! Yes, my dog! Don't worry, she won't run around, I have a long line as well as a leash and I'll clean up after her. She's a good camper," I blurt out, feeling like I'm at a border crossing and have deliberately withheld information from the guard. So I overcompensate and babble like a fool.

"That's okay we have retired greyhounds ourselves just as long as she's under control," says the woman behind the counter. "That'll be twelve dollars and I won't charge for the dog since you're only an overnighter you're in number three follow the signs it's on your right thank you very much."

I receive my change from a five and a ten and smile my thanks, marvelling at the rapid-fire speech patterns of Ms. Fleming or whoever she is.

"Oh Miss Brown I'm Lucy Fleming and the washrooms got good showers takes quarters and they're right next to your number three it's a good spot night-night now," says Lucy and flashes me a bright orange smile. I wave and smile back, thrilled to know her name really is Lucy. Maybe she made a choice to live up to her name, to pay homage to Lucille Ball her whole life long. How can I possibly live up to my own name, Mercy, when I'm obviously not cut out for compassionate sainthood? Why did Mother and Father seize on Quakerish virtues for our monikers instead of 1950s North American names like Doug, Brenda, Donna or Cindy? Those were the names we petitioned them for once, although we couldn't persuade any neighbouring adults or teachers to sign on our behalf.

I park and put S.B. on her leash. We start walking toward the sound of the sea in air as soft and damp and pine-scented as fine hand lotion. We're in luck. This unassuming little campground has beachfront and plenty of it. Shades of Home Sweet Home. The sand is hard-packed and the tide is out. There's less than fifteen minutes of daylight left and we march along at a brisk pace, S.B. sniffing and snorting at these unfamiliar marine odours.

Back in the van, she nibbles half-heartedly at her bowl of food. The travelling has dulled her appetite. I am not inclined to make a major meal myself so I fish out a tin of sardines and some crackers. In minutes, supper is down the hatch. Then I dig into the tea chest. I should set up the laptop now and send the neatly typed dream elements up to Norman first thing in the morning but I am too bushed and there's no phone handy anyway. I'll do it tomorrow evening after we arrive in Port Hardy.

Here we are. I pick up the green journal on top and check to make sure it's the 1929 one. I set up my big flashlight and position the beam at the yellowed pages, the fine blue writing.

I resolve to read only ten pages, to absorb her words slowly.

seventeen

NOVEMBER 13, 1929

We arrived in Vancouver just after dawn today and a cold, windy, rainy welcome it was. The C.P.R. steward organized the transportation of Ida's body to a funeral chapel here. I sent telegrams to her older brother in Moncton and her sister in Montreal. I could not find any address for her parents in her little book and yet it crossed my mind to send a message to Bailey also. Except why bother with the man when he's gone bankrupt and left us in the lurch as well? I do not care how he feels when he might chance upon a small article in a newspaper this week. I care about poor Ida and Chloe and Brigitte and Margery and myself and how we might pay for the funeral. We cannot pawn any more of Ida's good jewels. We must give them to her sister and brother. Margery conferred with the funeral director and they agreed to a cremation with a minister to say prayers. This will take place on the fifteenth. Margery pawned her own grandmother's jet earrings and brooch to raise the money. We must quickly recoup this expense from our dance fees and rescue her heirlooms.

While Margery negotiated this sad business, I managed to speak by telephone with the Orpheum Theatre manager. We will dance on the sixteenth and the afternoon matinee on the seventeenth as well as the evening performance on the seventeenth. I asked for an extra two hours of morning practise as well as the usual 4 p.m. practise on the sixteenth and this was granted. Brigitte arranged for our baggage to go to the Western Lotus, which the Orpheum manager recommended as a wholesome establishment and only a five-minute walk from the Theatre. Brigitte took Chloe to the hotel to get more rest and then Margery and I joined them.

Now, as I write, we are resting, each of us on a narrow bed and myself at the little writing table. We are quite spent, all of us. The tragedy, the necessary arrangements, the usual business of arriving to perform and now to think of how we must alter our dance pieces without Ida. It's all too much and we must simply rest and try to forget or pray for Ida's soul if that will bring some peace to us. I have a terrible, unspeakable feeling that Ida had gotten herself in the family way and was unsure of the reciprocity of her affections. Or perhaps she was sure no happy future awaited her return and she could not bear it. I cannot speak of this to anyone.

NOVEMBER 14, 1929

The rain still pours down and we are prevented from enjoying the Stanley Park walks we've been encouraged to take. Our heavy winter coats are quite useless in this downpour and yet we can't simply go out and buy other clothing, willy-nilly. We are not exactly content to stay in our room and rest but perhaps it is better that we thoroughly recuperate before tomorrow's sad ritual.

Chloe burst out with it today. Ida was going to have a baby! He wouldn't have accepted it, she told us, a very prominent businessman with a large family. Chloe is weeping inconsolably even as I write. She feels it is all her fault. She could not bring herself to discuss the matter with Ida and refused to ever truly believe what Ida had confided to her. Chloe didn't know where babies came from. Margery took her aside and explained the facts of life.

I cannot confide in anyone the terrible need I have to make a dance for Ida. It would be seen as shocking and sacrilegious. Perhaps if I thought of another name, something Greek, about a little tree spirit who ventures down to the village to join a village dance perhaps? This would be dangerous as she would end up on the bonfire in the village green with everyone else dancing around her. Oh, far too morbid, it will never do. Yet I want a dance that will endure and embody Ida's sprightliness. How else can I remember her as she really was, the saucy little girl I've gone to dance classes with since I was nine and she was five years old? That it should end like this for her on our first tour of the Dominion with so much more to look forward to, Bailey or no Bailey, is simply not right.

NOVEMBER 15, 1929

This morning we received a telegram from Ida's sister in Montreal and a notice of a bank draft to cover the funeral expenses and to send the ashes to Montreal. We all fell to weeping after we read this sad, final scrap of paper. Then we dressed, went for a little breakfast in the hotel dining room and took the streetcar to the chapel. It all seemed so sparse and empty and not at all suitable to pay our last respects to Ida. The casket remained closed. The minister was delayed and rushed in, mouthed some unctuous passage about lambs and rushed out again to preside at a wedding. I overheard him mentioning this to the funeral director and I felt enraged to have heard it. We sat in plush parlour chairs and could not speak to each other of the occasion except in tiny whispers about inconsequentials and then it was over and that was that. I trust I will not have to endure a day as dreadful and soulless as this has been ever again in my life.

NOVEMBER 16, 1929

The grey wash of this life is tinged, once again, with a glimmer of pink. We dragged our feet to the morning practise and inspection of the Orpheum and when we saw the magnificent stage and all the rest of this theatre, we began to cheer up a little. We spent the first hour in discussion about our repertoire and decided to see what the *pas de cinq* from Giselle would be like on its feet. This is the most worrisome as it is already adapted from a *pas de six* and the *Dance of the Wilis.* Three of us as the restless ghosts of unmarried maidens and Brigitte as our Queen Myrtha may not convey what is essentially a very eerie and threatening ensemble piece. Without a dancing teacher in the seats to advise us, it is also difficult to assess how we occupy the space on this lovely large stage.

We can go on with all the short pieces from *Les Sylphides* with some adjustments in the poses and *tableaux.* With Chopin such a musical favourite, we may work on two others of the short ensemble pieces if we need to drop the *Wilis.* The simple white gowns are easy to wear and maintain and almost every theatre has a good green forest backdrop so it is always easy to present *Les Sylphides.* The two selections from *Swan Lake* are likewise a pleasure to present and will lose but a little in overall impact with one less dancer.

I had to bow my head and pinch my little finger hard when I remembered how Ida shone at the linked precision dance of the swan maidens, her light, fast, bouncy little feet and her sweet gleeful expression during the final release of the swan maidens. When finally I'd regained my composure and looked up, I saw that every last one of us was streaming tears. Chloe spoke up bravely then and said we must dedicate this first performance in Vancouver's magnificent theatre to Ida. Then she asked if I would again do the "Angel" piece, as *La Chanson de L'Hiver pour*

Jonquiere is informally known among us since the Banff performance. I replied that I had eighteen minutes of ensemble work choreographed for that piece and had created eight minutes of solo dance when I thought it might be left at that or not done at all. If we were willing to practise the dance as an ensemble, I said nothing would make me happier as each angel has an extended solo turn.

I am interested in the dance having dancers and a public life. I do not have the physique or the temperament to be a prima donna of the ballet. I wish to create new dramatic dances, especially ensemble pieces, not merely for myself to have glorified solo moments. I spoke all these things in a great rush and then we all knew, including myself, what I most wanted to do. Create new dance pieces! A great black cloud lifted. We did our preliminary limbering exercises and practised for three hours solid, again with great heart and discipline.

NOVEMBER 17, 1929

I rose early and came down for breakfast with my ravenous appetite returned to me for the first time since we left the Banff Springs Hotel. Last night's performance was very well attended and today's matinee is apparently sold out completely with many Vancouver school children expected to fill the plush seats. The great Russian Ballet is arriving in December as part of their North American tour so Vancouver is very keen on dance these days, according to the Orpheum manager. We will have a short practise before the matinee and then work hard on the "Angel" piece in ensemble to see if it is worthy of mounting tonight for our last performance. It is stark indeed to write this. We have postponed a discussion of our future as the Prima Ballerinas of Mount Royal until tomorrow morning. We are hoping that we will be asked to play again at the Orpheum but with the great Russians coming soon, our chances are very slim. Tomorrow, as well, will be devoted to packing Ida's things and sending them to her sister. Tomorrow is a daunting amalgam of our past and our future.

NOVEMBER 18, 1929

Again, I am by myself at the breakfast table for some precious minutes to record the ever more dizzying events in our lives. A Madame Bleufontaine from Vancouver attended yesterday's matinee performance and left a note for us, asking for an appointment with any of us who might be interested in teaching children to dance. The Orpheum will have us back in the spring if we are willing and able. We are such a ragged little band compared to the full staging the Russians will do of *The Nutcracker*. Today is our day of reckoning. Margery is toting up the fees and so we will see what we have left after we retrieve her heirloom jewelry, cash the funeral expenses draft received yesterday, and send Ida's things home. Then we will reserve an equal amount spread four ways for our wages. That plus our return train ticket is what we have to rely upon. The sun is shining today at last and one can see the mountains of the North Shore from the room upstairs and now, the legendary scenic beauty of Vancouver reveals itself after these many days of grey mist and rain. This afternoon, after we get our financial bearings, we shall stroll through Stanley Park.

EIGHTeen

A SHARP CLAW SLASHES THE crown of my head. An urgent whimper follows. S.B. lunges up to butt her nose against my groggy head and to lick indiscriminately at my face.

"S.B.! Stop that! Just hold it for a sec, will ya?" I struggle out of the sleeping bag, grab my grey sweats and her leash and stumble outside in four seconds flat. When she has to go, she has to go pronto and I don't torture her with delays. It feels very early still, with a cool breeze coming in off the ocean and mist lifting off the land. After Sadie relieves herself, I reach back into the van for my running shoes. May as well get a little morning walk in now, while we're up, and then head out on the highway early. I grab my big black sweater to pull on over my T-shirt and again we turn to the beach.

The tide is roaring in, still an exciting phenomenon for us landlocked types. The sun is glinting through a bank of clouds to the east and the air smells damp and fishy. Sadie likes this reek much more than I do. Give me crisp mountain air and delicious tree fragrances any day of the week. Decomposing starfish, river otter poop and abandoned crab shells may bring out a hale and hearty response in others but I can't hack a steady dose of it.

Back at the van again, I assemble the supplies for S.B.'s daily shot, pull her neck skin into folds, inject the insulin and give her a dog biscuit. Then the dry and wet food mix goes into her bowl and I clip her onto the long line. Kettle on, coffee in the filter, 7-grain cereal burbling away like a nice clump of lumpy lava in the small saucepan. All's right with the world.

This is why I love travelling. The simplicity of my creature comforts. Waking up to a world that is new with a clarity that the same four walls of home simply do not provide. No telephone to jar me awake. I start my day when I want, end my day when I want, subject of course to the needs and whims of my faithful canine. If I miss a boat or a train or a bus, I wait for the next one. Freedom to be slow or speedy, to drift, to get lost on purpose, to explore, to dream. No one to inconvenience because supper isn't hot on the table at six or phone calls go unanswered or any of that stuff. Freedom is why I love freelance writing too. The fact that this expedition combines travelling and writing pretty much makes it a ten out of ten venture, in my estimation.

I jog over to the washroom with my toothbrush and shower stuff and two quarters, leaving S.B. to guard the van. There is one Airstream unit pulled by a big Ford with California licence plates and a converted school bus camper with BC plates in Lucy Fleming's fine little campground. No signs of life from either.

Lucy is right. The shower is terrific. I emerge squeaky clean and ready to acquire another day's worth of road grime.

We drive away with my strapless watch on the dash reading 5:45 a.m. No signs of life at the office either. I was looking forward to giving a cheery wave and having one last look at Lucy before we turned north. Sadie Brown puts her right paw up on the armrest and lolls her tongue out of her smiling mouth. I pop *Novus Magnificat* into the tape deck and we get up to highway speed with towering Douglas firs and cedars on either side. We drive slowly through Courtenay, a pretty town, where I stock up on fresh fruit and vegetables. We putter along the narrow highway, mostly beside the ocean, until we get to Campbell River, where I am tempted to stop but drive on to Sayward where we stretch our legs and fill up with gas and water. A long dark stretch of forested mountains, unbroken except for frequent clear-cut scalps, and the onslaught of driving rain make the next four hours of cautious driving seem much longer.

I love music. My tape deck and quadraphonic speakers are worth nearly as much as this 1975 Volkswagen van. I don't care about rain when I can take Ry Cooder's whiskey-voiced advice: get rhythm when you get the blues. I pop in the tapes every forty-five minutes and eat up the asphalt in fine style. Connie Kaldor, the Pogues, Michelle Shocked, UHF, k.d. lang, the Images Ad Hoc Singers, Kate and Anna McGarrigle, Stephen Fearing, Kashtin, Judy Small, Roy Forbes and Miss Quincy. They don't mind if I howl along. Finally, as The Mamas and the Papas and I belt out nostalgic hits, the little town of Port Hardy appears before my travel-weary eyes. Just a few more klicks to Bear Cove.

I can see the gleaming white *Queen of Hartley Bay* at the dock. The Pacific Ocean. This big ferry boat. Adventure alert! I have wanted to take this trip up the coast for years and now I am actually getting paid to do it! I pull into the ferry parking lot. Even though Lona at Great Northwest Expeditions said my passage was confirmed, I'm relieved to be here in plenty of time for tomorrow's sailing. Once established in the line-up, I park, then grab my notebook, camera and S.B. to walk some of the road into town for a good long stretch of exercise.

First, I take several shots of the *Queen of Hartley Bay* and hope that the weather stays clear for more shooting work this evening. I need an umbrella, I think. I don't usually bother with one but June is so often a rainy month and I don't like being constantly wet.

Ginger didn't flourish in the West Coast rain at first either; I know she loved Vancouver Island enough to live here for thirty years, and she was the founding mother of the Duncan School of Dance. I don't know what she'll do next as a twenty-four-year-old dancer though. Will she stay in Vancouver and teach pudgy little girls how to perch on blocks of wood? I think not. Yet their small remnant of a troupe is not likely to keep going with such limited opportunities for performance, especially with the Depression descending for ten long years. It is painful to know what's coming and to see that Ginger and the others don't have a clue about The Dirty Thirties and World War II and The Holocaust or The Bomb. Ginger is reading the occasional newspaper and has grasped that there are economic woes out there in the world. But they are, understandably enough, more than swamped with Ida's suicide and their own survival as an abandoned dance company.

Halfway up the long hill, we meet two surly-looking dogs who give S.B. the razorback stance and evil eye. We give them a wide berth while I think through the practicalities of popping into a store for an umbrella. Usually I can find an inconspicuous place to tie S.B. up for a short spell so I can buy groceries and such, but with dogs wandering around, I don't dare. She needs to be away from foot traffic so that well-meaning silly people don't try to pat her, especially ones with children. S.B. is terrified of creatures the same height as she is, especially unpredictable ones that poke at her eyes and ears and pull at her tail. I turn around. The dogs are following us. They really must lead an unexciting life if we're all the action they can find. I decide then and there that the ferry probably sells umbrellas; if not, I'll surely buy one in Prince Rupert or Haines. Somewhere else. Meanwhile, I reach down for a potato-sized rock and chuck it at the mutts following us. They scatter fast and we enjoy the rest of the walk to the outskirts of Port Hardy in peace.

Eventually we pass by a restaurant emanating chicken noodle soup and coffee aromas. My tummy rumbles right on cue. It is 4 p.m. and we've finished our tour of some of Port Hardy's main streets. True, there are no more dogs in sight but I don't want to leave S.B. tied up for long outside a big grocery store. It took us well over an hour to walk here. A fly-by snack will have to do.

I can make a decent meal in the van when we get back. I tie her to my day pack and leave her outside a little confectionary store. With a Granny Smith apple, one of those cheese and cracker packages and a long red licorice string, off we go again, downhill all the way, I wish, to Bear Cove.

We pass three little children standing on their doorstep watching us go by. They see a short, dark-haired woman in a multicoloured windbreaker and grey sweatpants being tugged along by a golden collie sort of dog. I wave at them. They don't wave back. The wind whips their long black hair around their solemn brown faces. I feel a little flicker of something nudging at my dormant memory. Dormant. Doorman. Norman!

I've completely forgotten about getting my report up to Norman! Never mind. There's still a lot of time. I'm sure I can plug into something down at the ferry landing. I'll flash my press card and speak in short, urgent sentences to the staff. It'll give me something to do this evening.

I don't know why I'm putting off sending the report. I keep forgetting about it completely, and am amazed that I'm not more bothered by it. Am I trying to repress the scary stuff? Perhaps what happens is Norman's problem now and I just don't take responsibility for it. Perhaps I have a sane attitude. After all, I don't have a computer program—or a mind—that makes sense of vegetable judging and some sort of military junta taking over a country fair. But someone, somewhere, might be at risk.

To work. Back at the van, I boot the computer into battery-operated gear and in half an hour I translate my hand-written notes about the country fair vision into coherent copy. Later, at the ferry office, I plug my modem and my laptop into the phone jack and electrical outlet respectively, and send the information up to Norman. The nice man working in the office waves off my offer of payment. "Official business," he says, and winks, one index finger alongside his nose.

I climb up to the big rock overlooking the terminal and wait for sunset. The sun sinks in the west and its long slanting rays turn the underside of a mass of silvery black clouds a gleaming pink. The topsides of the clouds turn dark purple, then the original blue skyline spreads out in saffron orange, pale shell pinks, bright carmine and crimson streaks. Sailor's delight. Photographer's delight too. I use up a roll of film.

The *Queen of Hartley Bay* glows like a white frosted wedding cake. Who knows? If the photos turn out well, I might be able to peddle some to the brochure people. I may submit some to the Image Bank, too, where I've made two sales to date. I'm not the world's best photographer by a long shot but I'm improving my eye, year by year.

The light glimmers darkly now and S.B. and I pick our way down the hill to the familiar green hulk of the Volkswagen. I am pleasantly fatigued and I hope for a quick descent into sleep, dreamless sleep, the better to rise early and board the boat.

nineteen

The funny thing is, there is no screaming or crying. Just the glum faces of the adults, the hushed babble of the children, several silent black and tan dogs, and saddle horses. All are lined up behind the log church on the knoll, along the edge of the two-acre potato garden. One elderly man, nut-brown and as wrinkled as a winter apple, holds a small leather-bound Bible to his heart. His eldest daughter, the chief, a stout middle-aged woman with alert, shining eyes, strides forward suddenly. She reaches down for a stick, one of a pile dropped when the childrens' game of Indians and Cowboys ended, and walks toward the brown river. The rest watch her silently as she jams the stick, pointed end down, into the dirt several yards from the water.

"Reaches that," she says, a little out of breath, "and we all move back." She swings one arm around to indicate the half circle of small houses facing the river. "Get what you can pack."

The sun rising over the high banks on the opposite side of the river shines in their faces. In one long, fluid motion, left hands rise up to shade the eyes of the watchers, except for the little group of five boys who wear identical black hats pulled down low. The river water advances to within a foot of the stick. The elderly man opens his Bible and riffles through the pages aimlessly. A lean teenage boy with a perpetual half-smile on his face whispers to the short, dark boy beside him.

"Lookit Old Man Ned. He's tryna find Noah in the black book."

The short boy's eyes dart over to the Elder, who is reading aloud now, though the boys are too far away to make out the words as anything but a soft indistinct jumble. The boy widens his mouth as if to smile at his friend's joke but his mouth is dry and he swallows several times instead.

The Chief marches forward to look at the progress of the water. It laps at the base of the child's spear she had placed in the dark brown earth.

"Rose! Look, Rose! The graves!" The short, dark boy points west, to a rise above the river where unpainted wooden crosses and small white picket fences surrounding the graves of children stand. The morning sun bounces off one freshly whitewashed and very tiny picket fence and makes the weathered and silvery wood from the old crosses gleam. A large tree smashes into the side of the rise, followed by still more trees, uprooted and swinging wildly in the brown torrent. A wall of water spills through the log-jam and tears away half the hill.

"Iiiiii-yooooo!" screams one of the women beside Rose. Boards and yellowed bones fly up in the air. The water rips into the side-hill again and a small red-and-black clothed figure is snatched up and carried off.

"Granny Ned!" shrieks Rose, losing her composure at last. She turns and waves the others by the church back and then she and the two women beside her make a run to join them. The water swirls in around their feet but they climb the knoll in time to avoid the next enormous rush of water and tree trunks tossed like matchsticks.

Grandpa Ned is face down on the ground with several younger people surrounding him, patting his shoulders. Nearly everyone is weeping. There are more screams as those who can still bear to watch see the decayed remains of their people and crumbling pine coffins sucked away by the water.

Three homes have water up to their front doorsteps now. Rose swings around wildly and points to the dirt road.

"You boys," she says, "take the horses and get up to the highway. Try and get somebody to come down and give us a ride to the Jackson Ranch. Go on now," she says, softly, as she takes in the stoics and the crying boys alike. The lean boy, his short friend and several others run over to the ponies and jump on, digging in their heels to encourage the old nags to trot.

"Come on," Rose says to the others and leans over to help Grandpa Ned to his feet. "Pick up his Bible," she commands one of his granddaughters. His wizened face is working but no sound comes out. His blue-filmed eyes behind ancient black-rimmed reading glasses run over with tears. He leans on Rose as the little group straggles toward the road leading out of the reserve to the highway. People carry their precious things. Babies in backpacks. School pictures of children, several rifles, a half-knit sweater and the rest of the wool, a toaster oven, a bareback riding champ rodeo trophy. Some newspaper clippings of Grandma Ned turning ninety years old fall out of the old man's Bible but a scrawny little girl with a thick mop of hair spots them and runs up to Rose with them.

"The men ain't gonna know about this," she rasps in her surprisingly deep, gravelly voice. "What're they gonna do when they come riding back from hunting in a coupla days maybe and we ain't here?"

"Tommy might know. He'll know what to do," says Rose. Tommy, her younger brother, left just yesterday morning for moose with seven other men and the good horses. Rose nods at the little messenger and sends prayers on to the men.

Take care of yourselves and come back on home right now there's bad trouble

The group walks past the two granaries, the hay shed and the lean-tos that the horses sheltered under in bad weather. The band's herd of Angus cattle, almost one hundred of them, were in high country still, getting a last good feed of summer grass, pea-vine and vetch before winter. Rose wanted the herd brought in before the hunt, before the chance of a big dump of October snow. Tommy persuaded her that the men wanted to hunt and besides he had had good dreams.

"Plenty of moose this time," he'd said, cleaning his old .303 rifle. She couldn't argue with that. People hadn't had more than a feed or two of prairie chicken for three weeks now. The fish weren't biting at all.

They walk past the long low roof of the cattle shed and the loading chutes at either end of the big corral system. The spring-loaded log gate takes two adults to open.

Then they leave the heavy contraption open in case the cattle come down from the hills by themselves, which they sometimes do, to great whoops and yells of welcome from everyone.

Rose is thinking about where the people can go when they round the first corner to follow the road along the river. The road is flooded for as far as they can see.

Grandpa Ned calls out in a thin, wavering voice.

"Galilee! We have come! No, no, the Red Sea, we...Look..." He starts to totter forward but someone gently restrains him.

From the far end of the flooded low-lying land, their young boys on horseback wave a black T-shirt at them. They are more than a kilometre away, separated by water. It is hopeless for them to walk across or around it. They'd have to go straight up the high riverbanks, climbing up the long, steep hogbacks and through thick stands of scrub brush. Too big a job for Grandpa Ned and some of the others too old or too little or too far along with a baby.

Rose turns to look back at the road behind her. Maybe they should wait it out in the church. The water would have to rise a lot higher to flood that. The priest won't like the people staying in the church, but it's the only building with a real cement basement and good insulation. The spuds are stored there, over his objections. Now the spuds don't freeze by November and be sick-sweet eating the rest of the winter. There's a stove in the kitchen there. They could make tea and bannock and hashbrowns tonight. Somebody might have a bit of something else, dried meat maybe. They'd have supper at least. Wait it out.

"Junior, Alwin, you run see if the water's up near the church. Real fast, okay? Give us a yell. Okay or No Good. We'll stay put till we hear from you. Scoot now."

The little fellows charge off, feeling important to do this job, even without ponies to ride. Rose faces across the water again, pulls off her blue and silver scarf and waves it slowly in a wide arc. A boy across the water waves his black T-shirt frantically. Then the boys urge their ponies into the water and come toward the rest of the band, hugging the shallow end of the water's edge until they run into thick brush and then the old ponies are up to their bellies in the murky flood. Rose narrows her eyes, says nothing. If there are no more logjams, no more big trees to swing near them, no big brown tide of water to panic them, they can make it alright.

The boys' crossing takes forever. The band watches them silently, not wanting to spook the horses or cause any of the boys to do something silly. Faintly, Alwin and Junior yelp in unison from the first bend in the road several hundred metres away, "Okay! Okay!" Rose pushes two of his granddaughters toward Grandpa Ned to start him back to the sanctuary, hoping the little boys judged the water level well. But she and most of the others wait for the safe return of the older boys on the ponies. Big-eyed and triumphant, they make the final stretch with the ponies having to swim for only six metres or so where the road dips sharply down the bank toward the flats. The five boys hang on like many-coloured leeches and the crowd of watchers murmurs approvingly. Up they come onto dry land, the bellies of the ponies heaving and dripping, the boys grinning and puffing out their chests.

"Big sign at the highway," says the lean boy with a tense, serious look on his features, swinging one leg over to rest on the horse's withers. "Bridge 151 and 192 washed out. Closed until further notice." He smiles his trademark half-smile after spilling out what he has obviously repeated to himself many times since first reading the hastily made plywood sign propped up in the middle of the highway.

"Ahhhumm," says Rose, slowly. Despite herself, a little smile plays over her face. "Good you saw it and got back safe. Walk the horses back. Give 'em a feed of oats eh? In the corral."

So, the band can't get out to the northern or southwest reserves either. Bridges are washed out in both directions. She motions with her arm for the rest to follow and they set off back to the church.

Rose thinks of Father Bertrand and how his white nose with white hairs poking out of the nostrils wrinkles up like a rabbit's when he doesn't understand something. Or when he doesn't want to understand something. This time, when he finally arrives in his camper truck to do his monthly service, he might find people hanging up clothes to dry by the wood-burning furnace or eating bannock and fried moose liver in the pews, and little kids running around the altar. Father Bertrand will look like the Easter Bunny then, his pale watery eyes darting all around and his old nose going like crazy. But then he will see the grave hill too. Rose grimaces and gently presses her fingers into her eye sockets.

Across the river, five miles upstream, Tommy, Joseph, Clarence, Albert, Fred, William, Duke, and Duke Junior stare at a small island around which the river has risen.

Eighteen moose huddle on the shrinking outcropping about two hundred metres away. The moose have scented the hunters on horseback and will not budge from the ground.

Tommy's mouth has gone dry after the first excitement of seeing the moose he'd dreamed. More moose than he'd ever seen in one place before in all his thirty-seven years. But the river is acting crazy, higher and faster than the biggest spring run-off. This is early October, when the river is usually at its lowest, easy to ford with horses in lots of places, good for packing meat across. Tommy licks his lips and leans forward a little, easing his lower back which has never been the same since he was bucked off Devil's Brew at the Fort St. John Rodeo eight years earlier.

"I don't like this here," he says to his cousin Joseph. "Even if we shoot 'em as they come out of the water, we gotta butcher, and pack everything across. Doesn't look good to me."

Joseph nods. They wait for an hour. The sun goes down. The water keeps rising. The hunters have to ride up into the higher brush along the riverbank where the windfall is tangled and thick and there are no trails. The steep shale cliffs between them and the moose island make it impossible to get closer. If the water keeps rising at this rate, they will have to bushwhack a trail up to the top of the banks.

Finally, the moose start to swim from the island. Some get caught up in a bunch of floating junk and there are terrible bleats and roars as they thrash around. The hunters curse. As darkness closes in, they can still hear the laboured grunts and splashes of the moose further downstream. Several disappear in the floating junk.

Tommy's stomach dry-heaves then.

TWENTY

I WAKE UP WITH A bad, sour taste in my mouth. I experiment with my tongue to air out my tonsils. Vile. Bad taste, bad dream. I have half an hour until boarding.

"These ones are full of people, First Nations people," I repeat to Norman. I'm standing in the ferry parking lot phone booth. "I'm getting on the boat in half an hour. But I want you to know that this river business is very much like the one with all the farm animals and farm people. And that first one, with the floating log and the deer. I really don't like it."

This last statement comes out more forcefully than I'd intended. The truth is I'm getting scared and would like to not have these horrible dreams with animals getting killed in them. The people part I can, strangely enough, distance myself from as if it were another violent episode of some trashy television series. But when I have to deal with animals getting shot in front of my eyes and their drowning and suffering, I feel sickened to the core.

Norman is still writing notes at his end of the phone. I didn't think I'd have time to get the stuff up to him as usual this morning but the contents were too scary to delay. There are two short blasts from the boat whistle. I hear people starting their vehicles.

"Norman, I gotta go, okay? Just tell me, is this like other people's stuff you've got coming in?"

"Yes. Whiskey Jack and three others have flooded gardens floating produce and buildings, and a couple others have First Nations people and animals trapped by water as well. I'm working on maps today at the office so I can spend lunch hour, at least, on what I seem to be getting here. Thanks, Mercy. You take care and when you get to Whitehorse, give me a call. I mean it now!"

"I will. Bye now."

I jog across four lines of vehicles, mostly enormous camper units, to reach the Volksy. It looks old and a little shabby among all these mega-thousand dollar beasts, even with only 60,000 klicks on a second rebuilt motor and an all-over paint job three years ago. I give a tug at the shock cords holding my kayak on the roof-racks. A-OK.

It takes four tries to start the motor. Maybe it's damp somewhere in its inner workings. Condenser? Carb? Whatever. The van is cranky about damp mornings. By the time it roars to life, I'm starting to get stressed out. I pat the top of the dash. "Atta girl, hang in there," I croon when the familiar wheeze and roar of the engine stabilizes.

Onto the *Queen of Hartley Bay* we go, following a Winnebago with Alaska or Bust, We're Spending Our Children's Inheritance, Drayton Family Reunion 1991, We Brake For UFOs and many other witticisms plastered across the rear end. A snub-nosed fur ball peers out at us from the back window. Then it's scooped up in a pair of beefy arms and swoops out of sight.

Sadie and I went for a good fifteen-minute walk this morning. We'd done the insulin, food, and exercise routine by 6:45. I don't like altering her food and exercise schedule because it's better for her worn-out pancreas if everything happens at the same time every day. This is where travelling is a challenge for me. We're getting up earlier and going to bed earlier than we usually do and that's okay. As long as her schedule stays consistent, she won't suffer from the shakes and staggers. As far as diabetics go, she's not in terribly critical shape, and I'm very grateful.

I'm still concerned about the length of the ride to Prince Rupert, eighteen hours non-stop with S.B. cooped up in the van the whole time. The one concession she makes to being a middle-aged dog is to sleep a lot more. This is a good thing considering what we're up against. At least on the *Taku,* the Alaskan boat between Rupert and Haines, we'll have several chances to go for walkies on shore during loading and unloading at several ports en route. Meanwhile, all those little fur-ball dogs must cope too. I've heard that some of them are trained to go potty in the same place as Mumsy-wumsy and Daddy-kins. Horrors! I admit, though, that there is nothing that S.B. likes better than to slurp aerated water out of a freshly flushed toilet. The best dog punch bowl around. She much prefers this to the clean water in her dog pail. Of course, my dog's unsavoury habits are not nearly as annoying as other people's dogs' habits. As in, *my* children are merely exuberant, *yours* are too rambunctious, *theirs* are completely out of control. *My* dog is a real character, *yours* is just plain incorrigible, *theirs* is a dreadful neighbourhood menace.

I yawn hugely, not bothering to cover my mouth. A sharp rap on the window next to my ear makes me jump in my seat. I swivel my eyes to the left, heart pounding. Someone in a uniform is standing there. I crank my head around and roll down the window.

"Lights are on, ma'am," says the handsome young man. I lean forward and turn the lights off, feeling my face heat up at the thought of having exposed my tonsils and molars so flagrantly.

"Thank you!" I chirp. He nods and walks along the long line of vehicles. I decide to take a stroll on the upper deck, check out the supply of newspapers, see what the *Queen of Hartley Bay* has to offer. I give S.B. a hug, a quick spine massage and a kiss on the white spot on her forehead. She pants and grins and her blue-filmed eyes search out the expressions on my face with such adoration that I am freshly overcome with love and loyalty. I give her another major hug.

When I first got her, S.B. was about ten weeks old. We'd cuddled up together in the van for the night and I promised her that I would look after her, no matter what, for as long as she lived. Then I'd cried my eyes out just thinking of the fact that she really would die before me, most likely. I cried for her and for me, two orphans on the road. In addition to all the good times, I have neglected her for days on end to do my work and to spend time with other human beings, including one husband who was jealous of her and vice versa. Worst of all, I almost didn't catch her diabetes until it was too late.

She kept losing weight and couldn't control her bladder and worse. I thought it was psychological. Maybe she loathed my ex-husband so much that she crapped in our living room to show her displeasure. She was banished to a big doghouse outside. But even after we left the husband and camped beside Ginger's cottage during the first round of renovations, S.B. couldn't control herself. It became obvious that something else was wrong. I gave her worm medicine, the most expensive dog food I could get, and nutritious treats like cold-pressed safflower oil and egg yolk mixed into her food.

She went from being somewhat overweight, glossy and sassy, to a dull heap of skin and bones. Several dog owners diagnosed it as tapeworm. More vile medicine. She grew desperately sick and so thin that friends who hadn't seen her for a while were shocked. I was desperately broke and kept hoping she'd respond. I finally took her to the vet's lab and just before those tests made diabetes conclusive, someone shot S.B. with a pellet gun from close range. I found the hole in her side right after she crept into the yard from a garbage foray. She hid under the porch steps and could barely move when I coaxed her out. Unfortunately, the thrill of the garbage hunt, another foible of hers, made for a nasty confrontation with an irate, pellet gun-toting garbage owner.

I called the vet. "It's diabetes," she said. "S.B.'s been shot and it's messy," I replied. Antibiotics and insulin. Somehow she pulled through it all and looks the picture of health now, except for her filmy eyes, which are another side effect of diabetes.

My buddy, my best travelling companion, my beloved old stinky dog. I give her another big, rough hug and she gives a big slobbery lick in return. Then I start up the stairs to the upper deck. The ferry glides away from the dock as I make my way up the narrow, metal stairs. Before I explore the inside of the boat, I do a good walk-around of the decks, stopping to watch the coastline of Vancouver Island recede and the shimmering blue-green ocean open up ahead of us. Again, a delicious shiver of joy and something like dread, the thrilling kind when I am willingly at risk, overcomes me. I dig my hands deep into the pockets of my windbreaker and head for the door to the inside.

I want today's *Globe and Mail* and the *Vancouver Sun.* I want to buy a large cappuccino, or, if the only coffee on board is machine swill, a large mint tea, and maybe a giant chocolate chip cookie. Then I will find myself a sheltered deckchair in the spring sun, pull out my sunglasses, sip, munch, and read for a good solid hour. Then I'll go down to the van and dip into Ginger's diaries. Have a snooze, perhaps. Rest up before I have to go into overdrive.

Everyone else roaming the *Queen of Hartley Bay* seems to be in the same good spirits as myself. I've never seen so many beaming faces in my life. These travellers are getting a jump on the regular summer tourist season and are probably congratulating themselves on that. Beat the heat, get ahead of the crowds, enjoy the locals before they get good and sick of tourist hordes invading their boats, highways, shops, and parks.

If Mother and Father had ever taken more breaks from the old back-breaking orchard and had decided *not* to go to Acapulco for the one vacation of their dreams, they might be one of the happy silver-haired couples strolling the decks. They likely wouldn't be clutching a Pomeranian to their hearts either. Instead, they'd have those little magnetic photo holders of their grandchildren plastered across the dash of their modest truck-camper. Mother would have brought her beloved tapes of Bing Crosby, Mario Lanza, Perry Como, Vera Lynn, and Shirley Bassey. Father might have wanted a CB radio to play with so he could yak with truckers on the Alaska Highway. The Grey Fox he might have called himself.

Unlike his big sister Ginger, Father didn't mess with the inherited Brown tendency for early grey hair. I have the first silver strands already but I like it. Being a short woman with black hair and a big nose and looking twenty-two when I was thirty-two meant being constantly underestimated by people. Now I get some respect for my advanced maturity, thanks to the silver hair produced in the wake of my second divorce. Being short has its advantages too. I don't often appear threatening so I obtain interviews with interesting, difficult people that big, brash writers can't get near for love nor money. I've also found that my silver hair, my good leather briefcase and my blue suit and pumps will get me past all sorts of pretentious snobs who wouldn't ordinarily give me the time of day.

At thirty-four years of age, I know damn well who I am and I decide how I'll present myself to the public depending on what I need to get done, whether it's buying rose fertilizer or interviewing a Member of Parliament (the fertilizer is free on that particular day). If presenting myself in business drag opens doors and allows me to get the interview or information I need, then that's what I do.

I'd rather be wearing my grey sweats, my gumboots and Father's old blue plaid shirt, and be nose-deep in my Tuscany Superb roses on an August morning. I'm not interested in spending thousands of dollars on clothes, year in, year out. I can write in the privacy of my van or my cottage, wearing a sarong, my moth-eaten housecoat, or my Writers Have The Last Word T-shirt and not a stitch more. With this line of work, I am lucky to have such choices. No. I made sure I had those choices. Luck has little to do with it. There is no such thing as luck.

My parents won their trip to Acapulco by buying raffle tickets to support some local cause or another. Kids' sports or a disease or an intermediate care home. It was the only thing they ever won in their entire lives. A pair of tired farmers goes down into early oblivion while old Nazis spend their declining decades prospering in North and South America. Where's the cosmic justice? The Great Spirit never responds to my rhetorical questions on this matter; at least I've never recognized an answer in the past seventeen years.

The boat swings slightly, changing course, and I am, as usual, lost in la-la land with my face in a stiff breeze, my eyes squeezed shut and a big, painful lump in my throat. This will never do. I blow my nose and make my way back to the steamy warmth of the cafeteria, trying to cheer myself up with thoughts of a treat, followed by the vicarious adventures awaiting me in Ginger's journals below deck.

TWENTY-ONE

NOVEMBER 20, 1929

What a tumultuous two days! The *Vancouver Sun* has reviewed us very favourably, describing us as "spritely mademoiselles with an engaging repertoire of classical ballet selections and a whimsical and delightful presentation, an original dance by a Montreal choreographer, G.L. Brown, of dancing snowflakes in Canada's colder climes." Oh dear! I suppose we could make wings of cheesecloth and silver paper and look as if we'd escaped from a school Christmas concert but I should be grateful that the reviewer read the programme and noticed the original dance at all!

Margery has announced her intention to take up Madame Bleufontaine's offer to teach children's classes. She will give it a full year she says, unless it is really *too* awful. Margery likes Vancouver, rain and all, and she also dropped a dark hint that her brothers might learn to wash their own socks and nurse her father now that she was this far afield. We had come to learn much of each other's private sorrows during these dark days of the funeral and doing the right thing by Ida and her family. Our Margery had worked cleaning houses for very wealthy people in Westmount as well as looking after all the cooking and cleaning for her father, who was mysteriously fatigued and bedridden ever since her mother passed away six years earlier and could do nothing of a day but write letters to the Editor. Something unfortunate had happened to the family fortune and her father had never actually worked a day in his life. Her mother had not come from a very wealthy family though. They have a grand house but can barely pay the taxes.

Margery had also to look after her two "occasionally employed" zoot suit brothers who treated her like a maid and on top of all these domestic and paid duties, she attended dance practise and performance with the rest of us at Bailey's for the past four years! All three of them complained mightily about the dance practise taking her away from the home (they objected to warmed-over supper on the hearth three evenings a week) but her beloved mother had long since instilled Margery's love of dancing. Dancing is the way she keeps her mother's memory alive. We all wept again, hearing this determined and yet so sad a story from our own indomitable Margery and thinking of our first night performance here for poor Ida too. Margery really must have an iron constitution to have kept up that pace, and now she wants to "rest a wee bit" and teach children! She is being very sensible and conservative in her planning as always, conscious as she is of where the next dollar is coming from.

NOVEMBER 21, 1929

Brigitte and Chloe will return to Montreal on tomorrow morning's train. They miss their families very much and cannot contemplate a working life other than another dance company at this point. They are young things really and not serious about life at all. I expect they will be married off quickly since that's all they giggle about for hours and they will make devoted and stylish wives and mothers I'm sure.

We each have $189.00 in wages after expenses and, of course, our one-way train tickets. I still do not have a decision made as to my own Life Plan. I do not know where I ought to live since nowhere appeals to me—the rain, the snow, both unpleasant—the world seems grey to me and I am not used to feeling this melancholy about Life.

I keep putting off writing to Mother and Father until I can be more cheerful. I do not wish to give them any opportunity of pointing to my ill-chosen vocation as the cause of all my woes. It would do me good to try and write a letter to George though, as just thinking of his merry grin and his Charlie Chaplin imitations makes me smile. But I do not wish to burden him with poor Ida and the dissolution of Bailey's as he is, after all, not yet twenty-one.

NOVEMBER 22, 1929

What shall I do with my life? What is it that I must do with these small gifts I possess? If I have asked these questions of myself once in the last five days, I have asked them one thousand times over. I do not know and the world regards me glumly, the grey-faced, fog-shrouded, endlessly raining world.

Except that I do want to create dance and there does not seem to be an opportunity to train or to practise here in Vancouver or anywhere else in Canada. It is not possible without a company of trained dancers. I would love to have such a company someday but surely one must have scads of money, an international dance reputation and an illustrious venue where the paying customer would gladly spend a refined evening. I think back to our family trip to Europe in 1924 and of seeing the great European ballets and operas in Paris, Milano, Berlin, Vienna and London. Those frothy confections, stirring and wonderful though they were, especially the music and costumes, are not exactly what I aim for. The stories are so very European, in fact, full of shepherdesses and princes and castles and we have none of that here.

I want to make dances that would celebrate the story of this country, Canada, a new, vigorous, adventurous dance for a country as vast and vigorous as this! The Americans, like Ruth St. Denis and Ted Shawn, are fond of spectacle and vaudeville and exotic *tableaux*. I enjoyed their Egyptian and Hindu temple dances when they came to Montreal. But I was also a little embarrassed for them, with their dyed-brown arms and legs and tummies, their très dramatic, anguished expressions and the *tableaux* poses held for excruciating, interminable minutes. The less than sophisticated in the audience (attracted by the somewhat revealing posters advertising the performances, no doubt) snickered into their gloves and scarves.

Brigitte and Chloe left this morning and Margery and I returned here to the Western Lotus after seeing them off. We enjoyed a breakfast together and now she is packing her cases upstairs. It seems that I will end up with the remnants of Bailey's props and costumes since I am, by default, the only remnant of the Company. Everyone else knows what to do with themselves but me. Will this self-inflicted gloom never end??

But my mind wanders, contemplating, of all things, the weather! Dance and the Canadian weather! Ice-skating, blizzards, spring's awakening, mountain peaks covered in glaciers, sheets of rain and double rainbows! Now these things are just as exotic as desert sands and snake charmers to anyone who has travelled from Canada to elsewhere in the world and sees this country anew with more worldly eyes. If only I had the resources to commission backdrops of great fir trees, the like of which I was amazed to see here in Stanley Park, with Fishnet moss hanging everywhere, and the Pacific Ocean and the snow-capped North Shore mountains. Likewise, a magnificent panorama of the Rockies and also the Prairies, preferably in the autumn when the vast fields are golden with grain crops waving in the wind, a sight I must see first and can only imagine now. I loved the great white horizon, the clean, clear blue and white lines of the world on the Prairies I saw from the train. I could not understand the complaints about "getting back to civilization" from some of the other passengers. Getting back to the slush and grime and clanging streetcars of the cities in winter? What else? (I must buy another book of blank paper to make sketches for these notions.) The Great Lakes with canoes and all the wild birds and the *coureurs de bois!* Beautiful Indian maidens dancing to *The Song My Paddle Sings!* I am brimming over with notions! Once I saw loggers in the Ottawa River seeming to dance on the logs as they separated a great jam in a bend of the river with the spiked long poles they used. I would have a chorus of male dancers (but from where? certainly not from Canada!) skipping from log to log with a lively French-Canadian logger's song for the score. Yes!

I must find a composer as willing to create these endeavours as myself, this much is obvious. The music must be inspired and positively captivating. A Canadian Vivaldi! I also need a brilliant and tireless costume mistress, a similarly qualified scene painter and props manager, and someone clever like Margery to make the bookings and promote the troupe all over the world.

Oh, silly girl, dream on, dream on! From east to west, a magnificent tapestry of scenes enacting the Spirit of the Land and the Seasons. I must travel the breadth of this country again and look with new eyes upon the landscape. I must learn so much about creating dance. But how am I to accomplish all of this with just $189.00? And a one-way train ticket?

NOVEMBER 23, 1929

It is presumptuous of me to think that with one eighteen-minute piece to my credit, an established dance company in any country would want to commission more works from me or even better, pay me a wage to work with them on other dances. I have sat here looking out the window of our room and rereading this diary, begun less than a month ago, for going on two hours, paralyzed by inaction. However, I am searching my soul and praying for guidance and until my own sense of direction is plain to my tired eyes or Divine Intervention occurs, I can only persevere here with pen and paper.

I am finding it greatly clarifying to rercad my thoughts and feelings in this manner. Perhaps I should apply to the newspapers and offer my services as a dance reviewer. Then I should have free tickets to see Les Ballets Russes and any others who come here! Except the gentleman who reviewed our performance has that end of things sewn up at the paper, I expect.

However, no harm in trying for there may be occasions when he is ill or otherwise unable to attend. Also, I might wish to talk to Madame Bleufontaine about contributing short dance pieces for the children's performances. I may wish to start with the children, developing my ideas as they develop their fledgling steps. (Oh, no! I don't want little caterpillars and butterflies! I want dark, beautiful dancers in deerskins and beads and virile loggers in open-necked plaid shirts and Scandinavian wheat queens and kings!) Try as I might to be sensible, I just want to dream of making new dances. I hear bits and snatches of heavenly music, I see colours and shapes and movement, especially movement, and I want to tell a story, to express the seasons and places of this country. I trust some sign will be shown to me, some scrap of an omen, so that I will know what on earth I am to do. Soon!

NOVEMBER 24, 1929

Margery and I have just returned from a successful search for a suite of rooms! We found a lovely place in a fine old home run by two elderly sisters near Stanley Park. We can do our own cooking and the bathtub is magnificent! In less than an hour we will have a cab take our belongings, and us, to Davie Street.

I had a bracing discussion with Margery yesterday evening as I had worked myself into a real tizzy and could not think straight. Between us we decided that it would be best if I stayed in Vancouver for at least a month and got my bearings. Margery will discreetly find out the status of Madame Bleufontaine's School and if there is work to be had in any capacity, she will advise me of it. I will endeavour to find out what I can about any other dance companies here as well as in Seattle and California. I must continue my own practise also and if I can possibly get some work managing props and costumes at the Bleufontaine School, I may be able to arrange an hour or two of practise time there every day. I am so relieved that we have arrived at this sensible decision. I can collect my wits, look at all the possibilities and *then* make a carefully considered choice as to my future endeavours!

TWENTY-TWO

I HAVE TO TEAR MYSELF away from Ginger's journal and remind myself that I have a job to do, a big pile of Alaska Highway research to sift through. Still, it's so comforting. It's her voice, her young self trying to figure out her life. I haven't heard her *other* voice or seen anything like what I *thought* I saw at the cottage either. I must have been mentally overloaded after that awful log-in-the-river vision. If I have to start hearing voices as well as having these prolonged home movie sessions, I may as well check into a spa with nice people in white who'll look after all my aches and pains and psychic spasms. Enough is enough, already.

I'm going to phone Norman when I get to Fairbanks and make an appointment to meet him in Whitehorse. I can't take a chance on missing him. I just want to understand how he pulls all this information together and to know exactly how useful we are. Plus, is he as nice as his voice? Is he thirty? Forty? Fifty? Sixty-four and waiting to retire from the Yukon government's cartography department so he can advance the cause of the Canadian Premonitions Bureau in a big way? It would be intriguing to meet some of the other people who send him reports from across the country. We could all fly up to Whitehorse to meet our computer man. Gather in a big hotel, have panel discussions, announce our successful interventions to an initially skeptical media.

I bet I'd be the only halfway normal one. I'd be there in my little black pumps and my crisp navy suit and my good leather briefcase; they'd be a bunch of crystal-fondlers and wild-eyed, self-anointed seers. The media would have a field day. We'd be laughingstocks on the late news, the kind of last-minute curiosity item the announcer presents with a knowing little smirk to perk people up after all the civil wars and pedophiles: "The Canadian Premonitions Bureau claims, among other things, to have stopped the barrage of low-flying jet plane flights over Nitassinan. This alleged contribution may come as a surprise to the United Nations as well as the military and legal personnel involved..." But what if? What if?

It's 2:20 P.M. and S.B. is still snoozing away beneath my feet. Time to see whether the seafood chowder on board is as good as the ads claim. Time, also, to see if we're closer to the coast and if it's clear enough to get some good shots underway. Where's my camera bag? Then, I'll have a solid Alaska Highway information reading session back here, to keep S.B. company and to get my head in gear for the interview with Arthur Flannigan of Tok.

Arthur Flannigan of Tok. What a wonderful ring to it. Great things I expect of the colourful Mr. Flannigan—fur freighter, trapper, potato alcohol distiller, and current proprietor of Flannigan's Stump. "At Flannigan's you hafta take the weight offa yer feet and pull up a stump!" he'd chortled during our phone conversation.

I thank myself for the two jam-packed days of work I managed to squeeze in before I had to leave the Kootenays, otherwise I'd be driving blind, waving my press card like a fool: "Gee, you look weather-beaten and feisty! Feel like being interviewed by a complete stranger?"

I have four major interviews lined up. Besides Flannigan in Tok, there are the dog team owner and breeder in Fairbanks, the flying midwives based in Whitehorse, and the retired Alaska Highway construction man in Dawson Creek. I'll dig for more en route. Two months exactly till deadline. It's not long enough. It never is.

The wild river research is much trickier. I fear I'll end up doing less than in-depth stories if I can't wangle a free ride down a river. The rafting companies are booked at least a year or two in advance and the cost is nothing to sneeze at even if I did manage to get in on a cancellation. Cost, availability, and time. Time to take a wild ride down the river, without Sadie Brown? I doubt it. Time to interview adventurous thrill-seekers, wildlife habitat advocates, mining and pulp mill developers? Maybe.

I climb out of the van and head back up the stairs with my tummy rumbling. The cafeteria is mostly empty, well past regular lunchtime. It's a glorious sunshine day and it looks like the boat's entire population is outside, strolling around or plopped down in deckchairs, basking in the early rays and the clean air. I order seafood chowder and a large mint tea.

It would be all too easy to lose focus on the rivers. The best idea might be to let the photographs of the rivers take precedence over text. I need to hole up somewhere on this trip to sort out the importance of the rivers. Tatshenshini, Yukon, Stikine, Iskut, Liard, Peace, Mackenzie, Rat, Porcupine, Kuskokwim, Tanana ... all northern rivers. Even thinking about rivers makes me uneasy with those river dreams. The isolated Native community, the flooding river, the country fair. Surely we're too far north for a country fair? Or maybe it's just another southern perception of the Yukon and Alaska. No quaint country fairs north of...the Peace River country? Well, I'll find out on this excursion.

But the marooned band, their hunters, their cemetery being flooded out and wrecked...all that could be up here. Despite the very tasty chowder in my tummy, I feel a little queasy. This all feels too claustrophobic. I reach for the small stainless steel teapot and pour fragrant green tea into the chunky BC Ferries china cup.

At times like these, I wish I had someone to talk to, just to take the edge off this kind of fear. It may be groundless. Dreams, so far as I can tell from the pop psychology I've skimmed through, are machinations of the subconscious, which provide us with a busy cast of characters or solitary journeys to make sense of when we wake up. Dream material may be much too painful to deal with, so the subconscious leaks it, bit by bit, into the clear light of day, mercifully slowly. Perhaps these latest visions of mine are just that. Just garden-variety dreams. Maybe I'm anxious about the wild rivers article.

My dreams are not only nighttime; some are prime-time daylight scenes. I can't quite remember how I daylight-dreamed when I was a kid because kids dream and imagine and invent and zero in on their truths all the time. It's hard enough to separate facts from merging into fantasy as a kid, let alone now, thirty years later. I can't talk to anyone about my dreams, except Norman, of course. That's what I really want to do when I see him in Whitehorse, just talk, without embarrassment or apologies, about all this nebulous stuff.

Ginger had her journals and she had her dancer friends to talk to about her quandaries.

Well, some of her quandaries. She is really starting to turn inward, to her journals, judging by the one I'm reading now. She had dozens of friends and acquaintances, however; postcards and gifts and late-night telephone calls all her life. She was amazing that way. Even though I've lived in the Willow Point cottage for more than a year, I've had my head buried in my work, or the roses, or the never-ending repair of the cottage. I haven't developed a solid network of nearby friends yet, the kind I've left behind in other places.

I head back out for the deck and see that the coastline is not clear enough for photo opportunities yet. We're still too far out in the Pacific. Maybe we're in for another spectacular sunset this evening. I walk briskly around the boat for thirty minutes, feeling a light sweat coming up on my back and my heart pumping in a reassuring way. Solid and steady. Time, now, to head down to the car-deck and start some serious reading.

Sadie Brown is dancing at the door of the van and she attempts to run through my legs when I open the sliding door.

"Hold on, Baby Dog!" I grab her leash and the plastic yoghurt container, a dustpan, short corn whisk broom, and a plastic bag. We barely start walking between the congested rows of vehicles when she ducks down and starts to pee. I expertly whip the yoghurt container beneath her, thanks to all those early morning tests when I was establishing how many units of insulin to give her on a consistent basis. I look around to see if anyone has their eye on us, especially anyone in uniform, but so far, so good. She pulls me around and we head back to the van. S.B. does not like the steady rumble of the engines underfoot, I suppose. She hops back into the van, I shut the door and make my way upstairs again to the bathroom I scouted out earlier. I quickly dispense of S.B.'s pee and rinse out the container, flushing it all down the toilet. Back down I go again, feeling pleased with myself for neatly and responsibly handling a potential mess. I wish everything potentially messy in life could be negotiated as briskly.

Ginger's journals must wait until I board the *Taku*. I pick up a pile of maps, my indispensable *Milepost* guide to the Alaska Highway, deservedly known as the north-bound traveller's Bible, and get to work.

TWENTY-THREE

IT'S 4 A.M. AND POURING rain. I'm wide awake and contemplating making a very early breakfast here in this Prince Rupert campground. My little nap on the *Queen of Hartley Bay* lasted for nearly four hours and then I managed a few more hours after we drove off it to this campground. So here I am, bright-eyed and bushy-tailed with no place to go. The *Taku* departs at 9:30, which means I have about five hours to kill. May as well finish these Yukon midwifery notes...what's this then?

Very yellowed, stiff paper crackles under my socked feet. S.B. shifts her front paws to trap the paper and gives it an all-over sniffing, looking up at me with raised eyebrows. I carefully take the paper from her.

A deep crease has obliterated most of the bold capital letters, which headline the small handbill. *Something, something, CONSTRUCTION COMPANY, EDMONTON, ALBERTA.*

> This is no picnic. Men hired for this job will be required to work and live under the most extreme conditions imaginable. Temperatures will range from 90 degrees above zero to 70 degrees below. Men will have to fight swamps, rivers, ice and

cold. Mosquitoes, flies and gnats will not only be annoying but will cause bodily harm. If you are not prepared to work under these conditions, do not apply.

This is not my research! I hunch over in the semi-gloom of the van, holding the old handbill up to my ceiling light. This is vintage Alaska Highway construction worker recruitment documentation I am holding in my hands. I have read these very words in no less than three publications from my stack of books and pamphlets. I'm a little giddy now. I can't help myself. I take a good, comprehensive sniff of the old poster. Tea and old paper. The journals! This must have fallen out of the one I was reading yesterday on the *Queen of Hartley Bay.*

I am thrilled. But first I have to put the kettle on to make my morning caffeine. And I have to dress and zip over to the campground washroom. Then I'll search through the journals until I find out why Ginger kept this Alaska Highway construction poster. Sometimes I feel like a real detective!

S.B. trots beside me to the washrooms in the lashing rain. I let her come in with me because I don't think anyone else will be up and about. But she starts to growl before I can open the door, which the prevailing sea winds are trying to yank out of my hands. I finally open the thing, and close it fast, but S.B. passes me even faster and she's still growling. I take a deep breath and come around the corner to see two bodies curled up on the floor.

Their big packsacks sport *fleur de lis.* I'd say I was looking at the raven-haired heads of two teenage Quebecoise. I clear my throat, "shhh" at S.B. and step around the comatose sleepers in their blue down bags to get to the long row of toilets. S.B. skitters around them to follow me, her toenails clicking on the battleship grey cement. I hope they have good cushioning underneath those bags. It's been over fourteen years since I backpacked around Europe; I remember a miserable night when a friend and I tried to get some sleep in a French city park bathroom in late March.

We didn't have anything sophisticated to cushion us from the smelly, hard floor.

As I finish brushing my teeth and splashing water on my face, I hear a rustling behind me. I turn around to see one pair of dark eyes surveying me and Sadie Brown.

"Bonne chance!" I croak, clearing my throat and towelling off my face and neck. "I mean, bonjour, sorry."

The eyes crinkle and the sheet drops to reveal a friendly grin to match.

"Bonjour, aussi. Avez-vous le temps?"

"C'est quatre heures et demi, seulement," I say, shrugging in a Gallic, or possibly just a nerdishly apologetic, way. "Excusez-moi, s'il vous plaît, et ma chien. Nous nous levons trop..." Here my rusty French deserts me completely.

"Too early, yes?"

"Yes!" I affirm in a loud, grateful gush, waking up the other sleeping traveller, who groans something unintelligible. I grimace. Her friend pats her on the shoulder and says something soothing about "dormir." I wave and click my tongue at Sadie, who is now trying to lick the nice traveller's face.

We hustle our way back to our campsite at a steady trot, avoiding mud puddles. The kettle is whistling like mad and the interior of the van feels warm and cozy even though there is no heater on. It's still far too early to give S.B. her shot, so while she settles down for another snooze, I wrestle the tea chest to the head of the bed where I have my pillows. I open up the van curtains at the back so that there is enough natural light to read by without eyestrain. Then, with runners off, I balance my tea mug on a sturdy stack of books consisting of *The Collected Poems of Robert Service, Another Whole Lost Moose Catalogue,* and *I Married the Klondike.* Then I sandwich myself cozily between my down sleeping bag and a Depression quilt made from men's burgundy and grey suits.

I skim through the journal I'm reading to where it's November 24, 1929, and shake it gently, upside down. Nothing flutters out except a tiny dried flower, purply-white, the leaves and stem now grey with age. Damn! I can't go shaking the journals like this because now I'll never know what date the flower was pressed or why, if Ginger doesn't mention it specifically. I carefully scoop up the flower from the pillow and place it back inside the journal, near the front.

What am I thinking of? The Alaska Highway was built in 1942! Why am I looking in a journal from 1929? I could be on a wild goose chase anyway and this little poster might just be a curiosity that Ginger enjoyed and on a whim, tucked into her journal. No matter. I count the journals. Thirty-two. None with dates on the outside covers. But there are numbers, thank heavens, on the inside front covers, from One to Thirty-Two! I'm in luck! Still, I'd better do this properly.

I wriggle off the bed and open up my portable filing cabinet. Under "L" there is a sheaf of label pages of many different sizes, some with colour codes as well. I'm a sucker for colour codes. I fish out the large labels that can be peeled off for reuse with no damage to the original surface. If I can make a cryptic synopsis of each journal, apply the label to the front cover, and get them all in order, then maybe, just maybe, I will come across some original Alaska Highway history in the making.

I may as well start with the first one. October 29, 1929. Winnipeg. The day after Wall Street crashed. (No, too long. Stick to the facts, ma'am.) Bailey's Ballerinas on Cdn. tour. Bailey's bankrupt. Troupe disbands in Van.

This will be harder than I thought. How can I just skim these journals and make notes that will encompass her full, rich life, and make sense?

TWENTY-FOUR

#1 Oct.29/29-Sept.4/30 Bailey's Ballerinas on Cdn. Tour by CPR-Montreal, Toronto, Winnipeg, Regina, Calgary, Banff, Vancouver. Bankrupt Co. Ida/suicide. Disband Co. in Van. Nov. Margery & Ginger work—Bleufontaine School. Ginger freelances—writing dance, theatre, book reviews for newspapers. Also choreography & stage mgmt. Aug. 1/30 goes to Santa Barbara, Calif. Denishawn School of Dance.

#2 Sept.5/30-June 12/31 Trades tuition at Denishawn for kitchen work at School. Loves California, many sketches re: new dance choreography. Feels out of place as mature student (others are 12-17 yrs.) Does vaudeville performance to raise $ for School.

#3 June 13/31-Mar.14/32 Creates *La Canadienne.* Tours with Denishawn Dancers to N.Y. Company chronically broke. More vaudeville! Who is G.H.?? (Love interest?) Many notes on new choreography. "La Cdnne" well received most places. G.H. "has broken my heart."

#4 Mar.15/32-June 29/33 Leaves Denishawn for Hollywood—works as cook on movie sets, tries to get work as choreographer for movies. No women ever hired except as "high-kicking, perpetually grinning, underclothed dancers." Tries to find movie work in costumes, props, etc. Doesn't "know the right people" is "too tall and too old" for "lecherous, cigar-puffing movie-men!" Often mentions being fatigued, "feeling low" & down-hearted.

#5 June 30/33-July 6/34 Leaves Hollywood for New York—finds work in 2 days! Acting in *The Emperor's New Clothes* off-Broadway. Gets small speaking role as English governess in *My Home Is Your Castle.* Meets Reginald Porter, English director. Gets another small comic dancing role (English fruit-stall vendor) in his production of *Aunt Velma Sends Greetings,* runs 20 weeks. Leaves for England on HMS *Queen Mary* with Reginald & Victoria Porter. Happiness! Career & like-minded comrades.

#6 July 7/34-Sept.11/35 London stage work, character roles as American(!) women in 3 of Porter's shows. Meets Edna Percival, master dance teacher & choreographer. Studies with Percival. Victoria Porter & Ginger create *Chimney Sweep Dance, Charwomen Dance, Bobbies on the Beat Dance* with Victoria doing costumes, set, production & Ginger the choreography. Opens May 1/35 in West End. *London Night Dance* panned by critics. "Vaudeville or Dance: Which Is It To Be?" (Reviews, handbill intact) Reginald rents hall in East End, charges one bob, & *London By Night* runs 14 weeks! (Predates Mary Poppins by 40 yrs!)

#7 Sept. 12/35-July 19/36 The Depression a constant topic. Movies (Will Rogers et al.) compete too successfully with stage shows. Several halls & theatres closed. Edna Percival dies. *La Canadienne* remounted, Reginald directing, Victoria doing costumes, etc., Ginger dancing with troupe of six women & six men. "Canadian Dancer Obsessed With Snow," "Attempt at Serious Dance a Serious Folly," "Our Large, Cold and Thoroughly Rambunctious Colony Presents: Dancing Loggers and Grain Harvesters." (Reviews enclosed) Ginger crushed by snooty Brits. Works backstage on costumes with Victoria on big musical, *The Bright Lights of Soho,* directed by Reginald. Choreographs several dances for show as well. Successful show, runs 16 weeks. (3 reviews kept)

This is fascinating stuff—our courageous Aunt abroad, doing original shows! I had no idea! But 1942 is what I need. Cut to the chase, Mercy, old bean.

#14 June 18/42-May 19/43 Loses her handbag containing $45 in Edmonton. Sees ALASKA MILITARY HIGHWAY CONSTRUCTION ADVERTISEMENT!!! Contacts Northwest Staging Line airplane outfitters, U.S. Army, dressmaker. Buys Victrola & Vivaldi's *Four Seasons.* Rehearses non-stop for 10 days. Performs at officer's party, Edmonton, June 21/42. Long train ride to Dawson Creek. 2 shows. Fort St. John—4 shows (not allowed to perform for black American soldiers living in segregated tent-town near Charlie Lake), Fort Nelson—2 shows, Watson Lake—2 shows. Meets Emil Beauregard after disastrous show. Works on new material. Flies to Whitehorse—6 shows, Fairbanks—4 shows. Meets Emil again, madly in love. Religious differences re: marriage. Living "in sin" at his cabin on Lake Laberge. G. pregnant, happy but often alone. Emil on trapline.

#15 May 20/43-Sept. 2/43 Ginger had a baby boy on June 20, 1943. She nearly bled to death. Baby taken by hospital nuns

> & adopted. G. not in right mind when papers signed. In hospital for 7 weeks. Emil?? Pages of painful, angry writing. (Nervous breakdown?) Aug.14/43 Emil's body found, long since drowned. Went through spring ice with full load of furs and the dogs. G. incoherent. Pages of "Why, God?"

I cannot imagine such pain. Poor Ginger. Such pain. I have a little weep for her. S.B. comes over and lays her jaw on my shinbone, eyeing me with such concern that I end up on the floor, hugging her and snuffling into her thick golden hide.

Now I know why those journals were stashed in a tea chest. Here I am moaning about a few bad dreams and not having anyone to talk to while poor Ginger spends her entire life, for all I know, keeping quiet about this terrible pain, this shameful secret.

TWENTY-FIVE

IT'S A GOOD THING THE ferry ride from Prince Rupert to Haines was a blur of rain and fog. I needed to rest and finish making synopses of all of Ginger's journals. I found a good campsite just outside of Haines and went for long walks with S.B. to unkink our six sea-legs.

Now I am driving the gorgeous scenic stretch from Haines to Tok with my sleeping bag over my knees and my camera dormant in the case beside me. All around me I know there are towering, spectacular mountain peaks, although they are completely socked in with fog. I drive slowly; chilled, wishing I'd added mitts to my list of supplies. I try not to panic about the deadline. Or mile after mile of fog-bound, unphotographed scenery.

I thrive on deadlines but a summer monsoon could seriously interfere with my ability to collect the images I need and I may need to drive this route again to do that. It's really not that far from Whitehorse if I drive to Skagway and hop on the boat from there to Haines. Or I can loop down on my way back from Fairbanks to Whitehorse. I want to give a sense of getting off the boat and ta da! Alaska! The final frontier, the exotic North, the homespun, the high tech...I feel myself getting rattled, putting pressure on myself. I cannot control the rain. C'est la bloody vie. Let's put some rousing Long John Baldry and Kathi McDonald in the tape deck and rock on to Tok!

TWENTY-SIX

ARTHUR FLANNIGAN, BORN 1908, RESIDENT of Tok, Alaska, since 1928: "In those summers we'd take the boats upriver to Fort Norman with supplies for the trading post there. We'd hand over the supplies, flour, sugar, tea, coffee, pretty basic stuff, and take apart one boat and sell it for lumber. Had no wood to speak of up there. Here we got wood. Wood far's the eye can see. Before we got started, we'd cook up a bunch of spuds, mash 'em up and freeze 'em. They'd stay froze until we put 'em in the frying pan way up the trail. We'd make bannock fresh and quite often we'd take along pork, slice it off and fry it up with the spuds. That and bannock'd make a filling supper. Oh, and for breakfast there was always porridge. Oatmeal porridge with a few lumps of brown sugar and a bit of powdered milk. That would stick to your ribs. We'd chew on pemmican or jerky for our mid-day food and keep on heading up the river, keep the teams moving. We'd use trails but mostly we'd use the frozen river beds to freight the goods further north. It was hardest on the horses. We'd leave caches of hay and oats for them to eat on our way back down and feed them all the way up, too. A lot of the load was horse feed but I bet they wanted a warm barn more than anything. Worst it got was fifty-five below during the day and seventy-five below at night. We had hay and blankets, didn't have down jackets or sleeping bags like today, just wool ones, but still. The horses didn't have it so easy."

Arthur Flannigan's voice gets soft and sad when he talks about the horses. He's a gentle soul under his gruff exterior. My notes are done, the tapes are terrific and I have three rolls of film neatly recorded, shot by shot, mostly documenting the leathery, photogenic face of Arthur. Two days with him meant sitting beside him at breakfast, sticking to him like a burr till lunch, and then coherent conversation seriously dwindled as beers went down his hatch. "12:05!" he'd announce. "Never drink before lunch." And pop went the first can.

The temperature soars to twenty-nine degrees Celsius between Tok and Fairbanks. I drive with the windows rolled down and glug mineral water at a steady rate. What was I saying about mitts? Will my photos do justice to the mountains and the great green sweeps of trees and the rivers boiling over the rocks? I'm now amassing little black film canisters at a steady rate. I find it incredible that I'm paid to do this.

Fairbanks. Trudy Reilly, born 1946. Life-long Alaskan. Champion dog racer.

So many beautiful sled-dogs, blue eyes, brown eyes, several with one of each colour. S.B. is simply beside herself when I come back to the van covered in more than thirty different doggie aromas.

Trudy isn't overly talkative. I observed that she really yakked up a storm only with other dog mushers, all male. My questions were naive because I couldn't get my hands on any decent background information on competitive dog racing.

"How cold has it been when you've raced the Iditarod?"

Long pause.

"Don't carry a thermometer. Probably fifty, sixty below."

"How do men feel about you racing against them, and winning?"

Another long pause.

"Some of them can't stand women doing much of anything except their laundry. But most of the men I've known since I was a kid and they respect me. There's more and more women competing these days so it's not like at first."

"At first?" I repeat.

"Oh, you know, the silent treatment or the poor-taste jokes when I was in earshot."

The third time I go out to photograph Trudy and the fifty dogs at her place, I spot familiar whitening dog feces on the ground. Then I notice an older dog with a dull coat snoozing away from the rest.

"Who's the oldtimer?" I ask.

"My first lead dog, Kluane. She's almost eleven," says Trudy, beaming at me with genuine friendliness. Finally I've asked something she hasn't been asked a dozen times by other southern journalists.

"Has she been checked out by the vet lately? Her coat's a little dull and..."

"Hell, she's old! She doesn't work anymore except to get the young ones settled down in their traces, to start training them. She can do that until she croaks as far as I'm concerned. She loves to work." Trudy doesn't look at me.

"I'm only mentioning it because I almost lost my dog to diabetes and I noticed some chalky white dog shit a ways back there. High sugar content or an unusual diet. Sadie's coat got dull, she started losing weight at an incredible rate...but now I've got her on insulin and she looks like a six-year-old except for the silver hairs on her snout."

Trudy takes a lungful of air and scowls. "I'll check it out," she says, still tough, but then Kluane stands and her ribs under the dull black coat are plain to see. "Never had any problem with that kind of thing before but I'll get her checked out," she says as she bearhugs Kluane. The grinning Samoyed-Husky's eyes have just the faintest film of blue-grey over her bright blue irises. I am positive of my diagnosis but I don't want to irritate Trudy by saying one more word about it. She loves that old dog. She'll get on the phone as soon as I'm out of her driveway; she won't lose face to some outsider with a diseased pet dog. I take half a dozen shots of Trudy hugging Kluane and thank her for her time.

Finally, here I am, flopped on a motel bed in the sprawling, busy, and thoroughly modern city of Fairbanks, tired and happy. The sun is still high in the sky at 10 p.m. because it's the fourteenth of June and I'm in the True North. I'll be around for the Midnight Sun festivities at Summer Solstice too, playing croquet all night in Whitehorse perhaps. Now, I'm bone-tired. My eyes are strained from days of reading maps, travel guides and other books, not to mention hours of staring into my computer screen, with headphones on my ears, as I try to organize my research, especially the stream of quotes.

Then there's the matter of thirty-two of Ginger's diaries. They ceased on August 31, 1958, but I can't get them out of my mind. I have to do something with them. Let the world know that there was a Canadian dancer and choreographer struggling in obscurity with great dreams and what sound like wonderful dances decades before her time. Announce that she is the spiritual godmother of the Royal Winnipeg Ballet. Send her dance notes out to Judith Marcuse and see if we can't organize a retrospective of Ginger's dance pieces. Publish her diary excerpts in dance and literary magazines. So much to think of doing.

I flew to Manley Hot Springs this morning, a truly splendid trip, courtesy of Trudy Reilly's brother-in-law who was heading there with an Alaskan television reporter. The pilot said, "Trudy says to tell ya her dog'll be okay and to thank ya for yer sharp eyes." How nice. A woman of few words and free airplane trips by way of gratitude. A doer not a talker.

I soaked the fatigue out of my bones for two glorious hours at the hot springs. I also shot five more rolls of film, lots from the plane. I have high hopes for them: wide angles of mountains and valleys, close-ups of dragonflies, a million wild lupins, Jacob's ladder and fireweed by the acre, the old log Roadhouse, and Five Star homemade dried apple pie.

TWENTY-SEVEN

Big blue wings. Green wings. Wings with orange spots. Whirring overhead. Someone is saying "Looky there, Albert, lookit them dragonflies, wouldn't the kids get a kick outa them?" Someone else makes little squeaking noises. "Frannie, Frannie, get 'em out, get 'em away!" She tries to brush the bright flies away from the long hair tangled over her thin shoulders. The big whirring noise in the air comes closer.

Old red plane in the air. Doing loop-de-loops. Motor cuts out once or twice. "Silly bugger!" snorts the big man in the silver brush-cut. The plane comes over the steaming water again. A boy says, "Awesome, eh, Jason?" The wing-tips waggle, the pilot's arm waves from the side window, there's a big sloppy grin on his face, and he hollers, "Whoooeeeee!" He dives, gathers speed, and then he's out of sight, past the trees. There's a thundering big bang, rolling like thunder does in the mountains. "No, no, no, no!"

Pure white silence.

Then shhhhh, shhhhhh all over like the earth heaving a big sigh and slowly a spray of light mud settles onto the hot water. No one says a word or makes a sound, ears still ringing, mouths hanging open like fish in mid-air nets.

TWENTY-EIGHT

I SIT UP STRAIGHT, TAKE a couple of good, deep breaths into my struggling lungs. Bright sunlight floods between the sets of heavy motel drapes. The digital clock says 1:01 a.m. I push away the blankets and head for the sink. Splish, splash, a little waker-upper. I don't want to lose the elements. I turn on my recorder and start to talk before the dream fades away in a puzzling jumble. I sink into the aftertaste again, the sense of futility, the numbness, the anguished bellow, "No-no-no-no," still a faint echo in my skull.

This dream isn't a long one. I'll type it out and send it to Norman in five minutes. There is a very odd tone to the dream...and this unsettling mix of emotions left over for me. I don't think I'll be able to get back to sleep.

Norman phones me back within minutes. I'm still trying to make coffee out of this funny little machine they have here in the motel kitchen. I should have brought my own thermos and filter unit in from the van last night but I was too lazy to get up off the bed once I'd stretched out. The telephone rings three times before I reach it.

"Bad news, Mercy," says Norman's familiar voice. "I'm taking an unscheduled holiday down the Highway because...if my mapping is on target, we've got a big problem."

"What?? Where?!"

"The South. BC, I mean. But ..."

"Norman? I'm well ahead of schedule here. Can you wait up for me? I can reach you by late afternoon if I drive like a bat out of hell."

"Well, sure, I guess. I can't leave until quitting time anyway. Why do you want to come?"

The voice is not exactly friendly. This is as deadly serious as I've ever heard Norman. No more computer games and cracking wise. He's on to something bad.

"You're on to something and I want to know what's happening this time. I go through all these scary dreams and vision things and you nab the information and fiddle with all of it. I want to know what the end result looks like. This isn't classified secret military stuff like Nitassinan, is it? This time you can let people know in advance, right? People can be evacuated this time, right? We can do some good with this stuff, right?"

"Right, but..."

"No buts, Norman. I'm practically on your doorstep, I'm wide awake, I can be barrelling down the Highway in less than twenty minutes flat."

"Well, okay. I guess."

"Wow! Where exactly do I meet you?"

"Corner of Main and Fourth Avenue at 4:45. Now you drive safely, Mercy."

"See you there! Bye!" I hang up with a flourish, amazed at my audacity and pleased too. Adventures for me and S.B. and none of this secretive classified stuff to fend me off.

It occurs to me as I zip around my little room packing up that I didn't realize how bothered I was by the hush-hush atmosphere surrounding the Nitassinan work until just now. I'd harboured an image of all of us, Norman's little receptors, as isolated psychic sponges picking up advance information like the white mice and other animals in cages that the Chinese observe for their earthquake warning system.

It's not that I don't trust Norman. It's just that I'm very curious and I like to have my big nose where the action is. I'm counting on having time enough to retrace my steps back to the Yukon from wherever we're heading in BC. I still want to sample the Takhini Hot Springs outside Whitehorse and spend a good four days at least with the Flying Midwives. With my overnight stay at Chena Hot Springs outside Fairbanks, I think I have the foundation for a very inviting "Hot Springs of the True North" article. It boggles my mind to think of the immense thermal pool underfoot, bubbling away, full of minerals, for millions of hectares. Is it piped into houses and offices, as in Iceland, or is it used in huge greenhouses all through the long dark winters or what? I must consult with a geologist, a geo-thermal specialist.

The old van is humming like a top. We pass through Delta Junction, Dot Lake, back through Tok, Port Alcan, Beaver Creek. The early morning is bright and cloudless, with a clear light unlike any light I've ever seen. I stop for a pee break and take a dozen shots of the Alaska Highway with shreds of mist lifting off it. The Highway stretches ahead, a long grey ribbon connecting cars and campers and big ore trucks with bright yellow pots on their flatbeds to another range of mountains. The hours and the Highway signs blur and I pass a man taking long lens photos near Kluane Lake.

Feeling guilty for having forgotten earlier in the big rush, I remember to stop for Sadie Brown's insulin shot just outside of Burwash Landing. I am flying low down the Highway, which is in very good shape, I'm relieved to say. A few frost heaves to slow down for, but they're easy to see in the daylight. I've also spotted deer, elk, buffalo, caribou, one cinnamon bear, and three coyotes. The scenery is so spectacular that I am saying stern things to myself as we roar (my muffler is sounding suspicious) through: "You must return, take eight rolls of film minimum and don't forget you are on a major assignment and you are chasing off to who-knows-where because of something nebulous in the night that may have been caused by an overly large piece of dried apple pie with ice-cream, you piglet! You must not leave here without going back to Dawson City," and on and on.

Here I go again, beating myself up for respecting my atrophied instincts. I am trying to be a Triple Type A personality when I'm another letter in the alphabet entirely, like P for primeval or S for seismic or R for receptor. Did Norman call the police? I can't imagine the response he would have received unless, unbeknownst to me, he has developed a respectful relationship with them. That would be a good thing. Police in all sorts of places call on psychics for tough cases, calling on them when the trail is cold, usually, but it's kept very quiet. It would destroy the public's confidence in methodical, diligent detective work if they saw some frumpy lady with big earrings and a bad perm being hustled out the back door of the cop shop prior to the solving of a nasty crime.

I stop in Haines Junction for a ten-minute rest and a stretch for S.B. and myself. I'm feeling a little weary so I mix up some Vitamin C powder and water, a good thousand milligrams' worth. My Never Fail Tonic. The towering ring of snow-capped mountains around us begs for photos but I can't stop now. It's already three o'clock. I build up speed again, roaring along (that damn $200 muffler is definitely losing it), slowing down through the pretty log buildings in the village of Champagne and past the turquoise and gold and rose coloured prayer houses on the other side of the Highway. A sign tells people to respect their burial grounds, row upon row of tiny houses honouring the dead below.

Finally, we're on the homeward stretch to Whitehorse. I will not have enough time to get this muffler looked at or eat a tasty lunch. Whitehorse has a terrific reputation for its good beaneries. I was looking forward to the No Pop Shoppe for the best café au lait in the city, according to several Yukoners I met in Fairbanks. Oh well, I have lots of nutritious stuff in the van yet. I am babbling inside my head now. Oh yes. I am nervous, now that we're nearly there. Here.

TWENTY-NINE

HERE I WAIT. THE WIDE sidewalks of Whitehorse are filled with late afternoon shoppers and tourists and civil servants pouring out of offices. I realize I don't have a clue as to Norman's physical identity. Then I do notice one man. He walks with a bounce, an optimistic, spring-soled launch from concrete to air and back again. He has bright silvery hair and when he turns to wave at someone passing by in a truck, I see a long silver braid swinging down his back. And the nose. A sharp, curved nose.

Now he notices me and his grin fades a little, eyebrows arch up over his hooded green eyes, questioning. He is much taller than I am, and he's wearing a blue flannel shirt and jeans. He stops a safe few metres from me. I grin at him and bob my head to one side. He bobs his in return. We must resemble prairie chickens with this greeting routine. Then the gap closes; we step forward and shake hands.

"Mercy Brown?"

"Norman Szabo, I presume?"

At that we laugh and laugh and can't stop laughing to say a coherent sentence. It's just so obvious, the two of us, peas in a pod. Then—sometimes I'm razor sharp, sometimes I'm unbearably, stubbornly slow—the penny drops. "We...I...think I should show you something," I finally say, still hanging on to his hand.

"Sure. Okay, but can it keep till we get going? I told the RCMP we'd meet them in two hours."

"Two hours! It's only two hours from here?"

"By plane, there's a plane waiting for us."

My head starts to reel and my heart revs up. I can't believe what I'm hearing.

"I'm not sure I can go on a plane. Or you either. Remember?" My dream from last night or early this morning flits by once again, the loopy pilot grinning and waving, the dragonflies so luminous, so pretty, then dive-bombing, getting into people's hair, getting very creepy. The big bang reverberating. I shiver and rub my arms.

"Suit yourself. But I've got to get to one of our people, he's right in the middle of it. We have the full support of the police because the staff-sergeant here has had a look at my set-up. He's open-minded and he's been around long enough to know that anything is possible, eh?"

"One of our people," I repeat slowly. My voice has gone all funny. "Like me, you mean, someone who sends you...whatever."

"Yes. Whiskey Jack." He takes a quick look at his pocket watch. "We have to make our move now though, Mercy. Sorry to rush," he says and points to the right. We cross Main, with me trotting beside him in what I hope is not an obviously agitated state of mind.

"I'll have to think about this," I say in a big rush, talking too loudly. A woman ahead of us looks back over her shoulder at me. I tone it down.

"I'll come out to the airport with you and think it over. Do you have a vehicle? Do you need a ride?"

"I've got my truck in the lot over here," he says, and there it is, a well-used red Ford right beside my green Volkswagen van. "I'd better take mine out to the airport or get nailed for who knows how many days of parking. You never know, eh?"

"Okay," I say, "I'll come out to the airport. I'm still not sure..." Sadie Brown is in her passenger seat, looking a little anxiously at me and this stranger beside me.

"Things have taken a twist for the weird, my dear," I tell her. As I back the van out of the parking spot, S.B. grins and settles back into driving mode, her right paw splayed on the armrest, leaning into the curves, panting happily. She's such a good travelling dog. Oh no! She can't come in an airplane!

THIrTY

WE MAKE A WIDE CIRCLE over the sprawling city limits of Whitehorse and then head southeast. S.B. is panting a little more than usual but she settles down and stops trying to lick the pilot, on whom she developed an immediate and highly demonstrative crush.

This plane is a gleaming yellow Cessna and I felt just fine when I saw it. Had it been old and red, something like a 1948 De Havilland Beaver say, and had the pilot worn a certain crazed grin, I would not be here now and I would have physically prevented Norman from setting foot on the thing.

"Tell," I yell into Norman's ear. Talking was going to be hard on the ears but I had to know. I hugged my day pack (insulin, needles, dry ice, toothbrush, toothpaste, hairbrush, wallet, journal #31, one pair of clean underwear) to my chest and leaned toward him so my left ear was handy.

Norman yelled back, "Whiskey Jack owns a ranch in a valley, very well-respected cattle breeding operation, and, along with three others in this same valley, he's been holding out on the sale of his place. Two dams have been built and a third has had its construction halted but if it gets the green light, his ranch and the others will be history. He's been lied to, threatened, offered varying amounts of money, and generally harassed for the last decade or so but he won't sell and he's organized the others so they won't get divided and conquered. A coalition of groups, everything from the 4-H Beef Club to the Historical Sites people, two First Nations who refused to be bought off by today's version of buttons and mirrors and the Direct Action Valley Environmentalists, has come onside and the media has picked up on it, nationally even."

I nod my head. I'd heard the interviews on CBC Radio's *Sunday Morning* program sometime last winter.

Norman continued. "Well, Whiskey Jack's valley is your valley, from your first river dream and possibly the First Nations village river dream as well. It's also Whiskey Jack's home and it has been for nearly sixty years. At first he didn't take it seriously because he often dreamed of things on his ranch that didn't fall into the precognitive category. More like him taking long, pleasant walks or riding on the ranch with his wife and one particular grandchild. But he's been getting the creepy ones too, with crates of vegetables and rabbits in cages floating downstream and wild animals drowned. This also dovetails into real life because this spring, a bunch of people from the nearby towns, all Coalition people, planted acres of land that had been expropriated and was just left fallow. They set up temporary buildings for small animals too. They're going to donate it all, wheat flour, potatoes, vegetables, rabbits, chickens, you name it, to food banks, after costs, and make a major media splash with it. It's some of the best land in BC, Peace River Valley Class I and II land they don't make anymore, and it's just sitting there waiting for the water to flood it or for some political will to reverse the dam-building frenzy in this province. At least they didn't put a golf course on it!"

"But why does Whiskey Jack think something like a disaster is going to happen?" I ask.

"He keeps seeing the flooding. And the flooding can't happen unless there is a structural fault with any one of the dams or an earthquake is due. This is a true earthquake zone, the one in Alaska in 1964 cracked plate glass store-front windows in Fort St. John, and not just tremors from Alaska, the Pacific Rim quakes. Really, it's too far inland to have much effect, although the local oil and gas drilling is being blamed for the strange tremors lately. But flooding? It's got to be the dams and we can't get the co operation of the fellows at the top. They think we're nuts and refer us to the RCMP who are already leaning toward our side or at least listening carefully. So, that's it in a nutshell."

I sit back and think. Norman looks out his window and then pats me on the arm.

"Watson Lake," he yells.

I look down at a small town spreading along the Highway, glass and metal glinting in the sun, the lake reflecting clouds, a bit of the heavens cupped in ultramarine blue. A convoy of tanker fuel trucks are lined up at a white building on the outskirts. Must be the café with the best coffee and breakfast twenty-four hours a day. That's where I'd like to be. My mouth waters at the thought of food and I realize that I'm ravenous.

Norman offers me a piece of sugarless gum and I accept it gratefully, taking one last look at Watson Lake.

"Watson Lake! Norman? Complete switch of topic here but I really want to show you something. Do you know any family or anyone called Beauregard in Whitehorse?"

He shrugs. "I don't know anyone offhand. Why?"

"My aunt was in Whitehorse in '42, '43. She...lived with a man called Emil Beauregard and I just wondered if there was any other family member still around. She, my aunt, kept journals and I've got one with me right now. She was a dancer and she was in Watson Lake entertaining the Highway construction crew. Do you want to read some of it?"

"You don't mind?"

"No, no, I'd like you to, really."

"I love old maps and Hudson's Bay journals and all that stuff. It's my job, eh, I get paid to read stuff like this." He beams happily, not unlike myself when I contemplate being paid to go on adventures and write about them. I hand him the journal, and I lean over to read it again, too.

SEPTEMBER 9, 1942

We landed on Watson Lake with floats on the Fairchild and it was something I'll never forget as long as I live! A clear, sunny day with the water spraying up on either side of us. The pilot acted as if he was driving a cab, so nonchalant was he! Watson Lake itself is comprised of a small number of wooden shacks and another tent town for the soldiers and civilians working on the Highway. I'm scheduled to be in Whitehorse the day after tomorrow so I will give a performance tonight and two or possibly three tomorrow. I've been shown to a tiny little shack next to the officers' quarters with a narrow metal cot and a washstand in it. They apologized for the latrines and I soon saw why. I shall attempt to have a rest before I rehearse in the space they have found for me, though I can't imagine what they've got for me since all I can see are these one-room shacks. Not to worry. My Victrola is safe and sound as are my records and that is the main thing.

SEPTEMBER 10, 1942

I danced on the splintery storeroom floor of one shack with the audience perched on cases of powdered milk, luncheon meat and pineapples in an adjoining shack. The men had shoved both shacks together, all the buildings are on skids, knocked out the facing walls and voila! The Watson Lake Concert Hall! They spread gunnysacks over the roof to keep out the drafts and arranged the boxes of canned goods into a bank of raised seats. Very ingenious I thought. Last night's performance was attended by over fifty men. The commander of the Americans insisted on posting a guard outside my door all night. I am grateful for the gesture though I didn't imagine I'd be in danger. This is the most uncivilized-looking camp I've been in. Fort St. John and Fort Nelson look like established cities by comparison, wooden sidewalks or not. But the scenery in Watson Lake is marvellous, true wilderness and huge blue skies. My spirits expand to match the horizon.

This afternoon I danced a 4 p.m. performance with snow starting to fall outside. The men looked glum so I did a vaudeville sort of thing after the usual selections and that seemed to cheer them up a little. Many of them look exceedingly tired and the talk is that the Highway is very near to completion further north.

SEPTEMBER 11, 1942

I left Watson Lake early this morning in such a state of shock and excitement and confusion. The performance at seven last night was fine but the nine o'clock final show was, without a doubt, the most disastrous of my entire career. By then it had snowed two feet and there must have been eighty men crammed into the place with several rows on the floor, encroaching on my tiny bit of space. I had to look sharp and confine myself to the far end for the larger movements or else I'd be stamping all over them. It was so warm, with all those people, that the door from "my" building was left open, creating a chilly draft. I began with my four Canadian Seasons pieces and the Vivaldi, which I shall record here for posterity for when I recover I shall write a humorous piece and send it out for publication after we win the War. First, *Spring Run-off in the Rockies*, then *Summer Solstice in Saskatchewan*, followed by *Moody Manitoba Mists of Autumn*, and finally that old chestnut, *La Chanson de L'Hiver pour Jonquiére.*

I wasn't terribly well received by this audience, to put it mildly. I could hear a low rumble of chatter throughout, which was very disconcerting and I had to apply myself so as not to lose my concentration. Two young fellows in the front row on the floor chewed gum the whole while, like a pair of moose chewing their cuds and making loud smacking noises. Really, I can't abide the habit of gum chewing. Then I began the contemplative middle piece, another original work, *Soliloquy for Susannah.* I should have known this was a mistake. I ought to have done a vaudeville sketch. I was no more than two minutes progressed with this dance when the yelling started. "Take it off! Change the music! Speed it up lady!" Then the terrible chanting started, "Take it off, take it off" and coins were being tossed at me and one landed on my Victrola. There was a hideous sound as it wedged up against the needle. No one in charge seemed to be in the place and I became frightened though I tried not to show it. I turned my back to them and with shaking hands, managed to get the two-bits off my Chopin record so that it wouldn't be rendered completely unplayable. Then I put the lid on and clipped it shut. All the while there was this terrible din and stomping and clapping and "Show us yer tits" et cetera. Then silence.

When I turned around to face them again, with the idea of walking right out the door, quick march, with my Victrola safely in my arms, there was a man with his back to me. He was facing that unruly lot, a great, strapping fellow in full winter gear so he looked even more imposing with a full-length buffalo coat and big felt-pack boots. I can still see the two gum-chewers with their mouths hanging open and the whites of their eyes gleaming, staring up at this mountain of a man. He pointed at the door I myself was planning to escape through and said in a very calm voice, "Out." And they did, all those soldiers, leaving a trail of sour alcohol vapours behind them.

When he turned around, I saw why they left. A more fierce-looking individual I'm not ever likely to see. Half his face had been clawed by some animal, a wolverine, he said later, and his eyes were so dark they were black. Then he said, in a shy, hesitant manner, "Would you care to dance, ma'am?" He smiled, finally, a very sweet smile and I nodded, still in shock, set the box down and we did a sort of dance to the Chopin, not a waltz exactly but easy enough to follow, for a long time. The two-step, he calls it. This is Emil Beauregard and he is French and Tahltan and Scottish and Carrier and I will see him again in Whitehorse. He is an aeroplane engine mechanic and works for the Northwest Staging Line but he has a cabin and a trapline near Lake Laberge. When he smiles, he is transformed from a craggy, horribly scarred villain to a most appealing man, and certainly a hero, in my eyes. I don't know if I would have been able to walk away from that drunken crowd. I shudder to imagine that scene further. Suffice to say my heart is simply, completely, absolutely smitten. We talked and danced until 4 a.m. and now I must wait for one more week to see him. Thus ends the record of the very worst performance and most wonderful, magical evening of my life!

Norman closes the small green book and looks at me, puzzled. "Okay! Emil Beauregard," I say. "Beauregard," I repeat, upping the volume, noticing the blank look in his eyes.

"I don't, personally, know any Beauregards. But I think there's a family by that name in Telegraph Creek. I think." He slowly settles back in his seat.

I wait for more words from him.

"Mercy, I still don't get it. I mean, this is your aunt's diary and she was doing dance shows for the Highway building troops and...so?"

"So, I think...but without hospital records, it'll be hard to prove... that you're Ginger and Emil's son. You're my cousin! Look how our hair is prematurely greying, silvering, whatever! Look at these noses! And if I showed you a colour photo of Ginger, you'd see how you have her green eyes. Identical!"

I am yelling again, competing with the Cessna's engine. Norman looks shocked.

"No, that's not possible, Mercy. Hold on now. I've still got a Hungarian father and mother back there in Whitehorse!"

But he starts to leaf through Ginger's journal, flipping the pages, not saying a word, reading quickly. I keep a muzzle on, thinking about a million possibilities, including the fact that a good many women, single and married, had the babies of American soldiers during the construction of the Alaska Highway. Maybe Norman is one of those, after all. But I'm conveniently ignoring the fact that he has his own parents, aren't I? Still, he is flapping through those diary pages at a fast pace.

"Did Ginger ever get married again?" he asks.

I jump, not expecting the sound of his voice in the middle of these reveries.

"No. Not as far as I know. She opened a dance school in Duncan, on Vancouver Island. Taught there for thirty years until she retired and came to live near her brother's family who carried on the family orchard. The brother was my father. I didn't know about any of this stuff, about Ginger being up North. It's kind of like a missing year in her life or a year no one in my family talked about, if they knew of it at all. I'm sorry about coming on so strong about you being her son and all that. I took a blind leap over a stack of assumptions. You know how it is."

"Yeah, it's okay. Really, it is. Maybe we can do a bit of digging, hospital records for a start, when we get back to Whitehorse, eh?"

I nod and smile at his gracious deferring of my blundering. He is a nice man. I'd have liked him to be my cousin. Oh well. I look down again. The Highway carves its way through an endless boreal carpet, dotted here and there with gas rigs and one section of clear-cut brown squares. The forest abruptly gives way to huge fields, green, brown, and light gold rectangles and squares and L-shapes. The farm buildings are miles apart, or so it seems from the air. I am used to the dense cluster of orchards and hobby farms of my own stomping grounds. This is the northern prairie, complete with miniature grain elevators and railcars.

THIRTY-one

OUR PILOT CIRCLES OVER THE airstrip, listening to a series of squawks on his radio. He makes another circle and growls back into the radio before signing off and bringing us in on a beautifully smooth landing. We taxi over to the hangar and come to a stop. My ears gratefully soak up the sudden silence.

"Guess you heard that, eh?" He turns around, ruffling Sadie Brown's ears, leaning toward us.

"No," we chorus in unison.

"Well, now. Just came over the blower. Some nut in a plane's gone and dumped nitro or something on those pulp mills in Alberta, those big ones being built by the Japanese down river?"

"Oh damn," Norman swears softly. My mouth is open and I can feel my forehead tightening up. We're too late.

"Did anybody...die?" I finally get the words out.

"Didn't say. They were on strike there, I know that, and it happened just a few minutes ago. Don't know if they had any outside crews brought in to work a Friday evening shift but it don't seem likely. Ain't that something?" He turns back around. "Surely to God those protesters wouldn't bomb the place, would they? They asked if I'd seen an old red plane..."

"An old De Havilland Beaver?" I interrupt.

He swings around again, looking at me very suspiciously. "How'd you know? Norman? What the heck's going on here?"

"Oh," says Norman, "Oh, she's a...journalist but..."

"You been talking to those environmentalists? That's who I'd be looking into, if I was the cops," our pilot declares, still giving me the unfriendly eye.

"No, no. It's nothing like that. It's a long story but really, I've been researching old planes and bush pilots and...things like that so that's why, it just popped out," I manage to say, sounding perky near the end so he'd think I was just trying to show off my research instead of being a compulsive blabbermouth.

"Oh? Well! That's different! Who ya working for? Maybe I could help you out there. See, I know this great old guy, used to work up here..." We climb out of the Cessna onto asphalt, which is shimmering with heat waves and feels like forty degrees Celsius. Our camaraderie restored, I trot along beside the pilot, taking notes and names all the way to the hangar.

An older man and woman stand beside a maroon truck in the parking lot and Norman, walking quickly, steers us over toward them. He always seems to walk quickly.

"You heard?" says the man, holding his hand out for Norman to shake.

"The bombing?"

"Yes. We just got it on the radio, no details. This is Mercy Brown?" the man asks.

"Right! Mercy, this is Della and Rex Westman. Rex is the contact I told you about. Whiskey Jack." We shake hands and smile at each other but we're all silent and looking a bit strained.

Norman plunges in. "I don't know if we're too late. We might have come down for nothing it seems. I got the word out to the police in the middle of last night. Is the up-river reserve evacuated, do you happen to know?"

Rex nods. "That's done and they moved the people on either side of the river on the upper stretch. A couple ranches and one sand and gravel operation, they're all out, safe. Livestock got moved too. The army was up here on manoeuvres so they were called in on this, real handy they were here. Hundreds of 'em with trucks and jeeps, hauled a lot of folks and animals out in a big hurry."

I cannot stop myself. "Did the army sand-bag around the cemetery at the reserve?"

"Yes, they did do that, I heard."

Norman allows a quick tight smile to cross his face then. "And the 4-H Fair? Was that moved somewhere else?"

Rex nods again. "Well away from the river. That's a good thing too. Finally got Hydro to make some official statement so people wouldn't get right spooked but they'd still take it seriously enough to co-operate and get moving."

Norman looks hopeful. "Aren't we in the clear here then?"

Rex shakes his head, pulls off his green John Deere cap and rubs his gleaming scalp. "No," he says slowly, flushing red. "I think there's more to come. What I saw, you know, I kind of saw there...was the wood flying like matchsticks." He looks up, hesitating, waiting. Norman nods vigorously. "Then the flying dirt and water." Rex stops again, looking up.

I grab Norman by the arm. "Flying dirt!" Norman nods. I look at Rex, who is looking very uncomfortable, a deep red stain of embarrassment still lurking under his nut-brown tan.

Who'd ever think it? Rex is so tanned and weather-beaten, he could star in an ad for preserving the nation's family farms. With combines going flat-out all day and all night under a full moon to get the crop off before it rains. With grandparents who worked on barn-raisings, threshing gangs, quilting bees. Whiskey Jack. Another seismic receptor. Just a fine ordinary hard-working farmer. We are all quiet for a moment. Far away, we hear the drone of another airplane and from a slough nearby, the sweet gurgle of a red-winged blackbird. My nose twitches as a gust of hot wind brings me melting tar, cut clover, and a combination of wild flowers. There are a few vehicles in the parking lot but the small terminal is closed. The sun is high in the sky. Summer, glorious mid-summer. And here we are in the middle of who-knows-what with no clues to proceed, it seems.

The droning plane comes closer and the sun bounces off the glass. For lack of anything better to do, we stand here looking up at it. The plane circles once as if preparing for landing. I grab Norman's arm. He looks at me then, despair in every pore. There is no need to speak. It is an old red De Havilland Beaver.

It banks sharply and comes straight toward us, flying less than thirty metres above the runway. The pilot waves, leaning out of the open side window, his mouth opening and closing. He's yelling at us but we can't hear above the roar of the engine. He pulls up, waggling his wings, and veers west.

This time Della speaks. "It's Ted, alright," she says. "You thought it was him, didn't you, luv?" Her small hand pats her husband's big knuckles. Rex hangs his head, shaking it from side to side like a wounded buffalo. A bald wounded buffalo.

"We got ourselves trouble," he says finally. He jams the cap back down on his head. "And I know just where he's headed next! Norman, it's like you figured. He's gonna try and blow it all to hell." He spreads his hands out, looking pained and apologetic. Then he sprints, with surprising speed for such a big man, to their truck and is gone, speeding away before the rest of us can collect our wits.

"Well," chirps Della. "That's all very well, you great silly git, but you've gone and left us with no visible means of transport."

We groan in unison, Norman and I. Della spots a pickup leaving and waves wildly at it. Our pilot and a buddy from the small plane hangar are heading into town. Norman hops in with them, hollering something about finding a rent-a-car for us in town or the main airport.

Della and I head for a clump of poplar trees under which sits a wooden picnic table.

"Tell me about Ted," I ask, after we sit down. I am feeling very tired and useless. Too much excitement for two days and less than seven hours' sleep in total. My eyes are so poached in this heat that they ache in their sockets. I dig out my sunglasses, finally, gratefully, remembering I'd packed them. "Shouldn't we phone the police? How can an old truck and a rent-a-car catch up to an airplane, for Pete's sakes?"

"Rex has a CB in the truck," says Della. "I could see him barking into it before he even left the parking lot."

"But why couldn't we have gone with him?" I say, hearing a whine creep into my voice.

"It's a family matter," says Della, almost primly, as if I'd asked her about feminine hygiene products. She leans toward me, one finger up against her small, pointy nose.

"He's the older brother to Rex. There's just the two of them and he's a real nutter. I wouldn't say this around Rex, mind, but they're as different as night and day. I didn't meet his brother until I came out from England after the war in '46. Ted hadn't flown in the war, he'd been infantry like Rex. He was one of the ones who got ruined by it, the war. Not one of the quiet, depressed ones, like some of the boys. Awful, really. No, Ted came out of it with some kind of urge to kill himself, if you ask me. My Rex swears Ted was quiet and decent and all that before the war but he came out of it all full of himself, braggy and swaggering. Well, he never actually fought, you know. He was a tank mechanic, very clever that way, kept all the machines rolling along. To hear him talk, you'd think it was one big party, French girls swarming all over them, casks of wine, oh yes."

"But what's he up to now? Flying this plane around?" I manage to get a word in edgewise while Della blows her nose.

"Oh! Now he tells folks that are none the wiser that he was a regular flying ace, him and Billy Bishop, just like this!" She crosses two fingers, waggling them impatiently. "Not in front of Rex or I, mind, but the stories get 'round to us, you know. All talk, none of it true. No. Ted's hobby is planes, he likes restoring them. Learned to fly them back east, right after the war. He's clever with mechanics, he is. I said that already. Well. He's worked for every garage around, lasts a few months until they get right sick of him or he goes on a bender, gets smashed up and that's the end of that job." She leans forward and whispers. "Father was the same. Like father, like son." She draws one finger across her throat and settles back, nodding emphatically.

"What do you mean?" I sit up straight.

"Father was a bad-tempered lot one minute, and sweet as can be the next. Rex told me that. Rex talked to his doctor some years back after one of Ted's accidents. Our doctor is not a qualified psychiatrist by any means but he's good, he's seen a lot in his time and he keeps up with the medical research, you know? Says that Ted, and his father before him after World War I, developed the same kind of battle fatigue, he called it, not just shell shock as if all it was about were loud noises setting them off, though they do that, too. But this fatigue is a mental thing, it made them jumpy and on edge, nightmares, the like. Ted tries but he tries too hard, in a way. Big plans for the future, castles in the air, like, races around laughing his head off for weeks on end, then bang. Goes on a bender, cracks himself up, ends up in hospital with some accident every single time, depressed for weeks, blaming the rest of the world for his woes. He won't stay on the medication either. He goes off it because he's feeling good again. Then he goes on the skids promptly and hasn't figured it out yet. Awful frustrating. If you ask me, he knows hospital's the safest place for him. He's had three wives, you know." Della powders her face with quick little pats, using a small tortoiseshell compact.

"But suicide?" I urge her on again.

"Ted found him out in the bush. Father had a trapline, see, and he was about to lose all of it underwater with that first dam on the river? Well, their father couldn't imagine himself another life other than the bush. The boys had gone on to other things after the war,

Rex ranching and Ted in town at one garage or another. But their father liked his independence. Stayed in his little log place miles from anywhere. Well. He didn't come in for spring supplies and that didn't make sense at all. So Ted went out to see what was what and found him where he'd hung himself. Animals had been at him. Affected Ted something awful. Went on a terrible binge after that. Rex was sad and all that but Rex didn't idolize his father like Ted did. Rex remembers the leather strap and his terrible moods and then his acting like nothing had ever happened, playing his button accordion all night, singing away. Rex barely remembers his mother, she died when he was six or seven, but he remembers her well, a kind, quiet woman. Rex must take after her, he's a lovely natured man, he truly is. Well, here's Norman."

"Yes!" I say, grateful for the sight of the rental car. My ears are ringing and my senses are overloaded.

"Della, we probably should head out to your ranch if Rex is going to be near there. I have to talk with him about this..." Norman's voice trails off. I grab S.B. by the collar and we all pile into the car.

"Well, if you ask me," pipes Della from the back seat, "he's gone out to the new dam site. That's just out past our farm, mind, but Ted's been ranting and raving about that for years. He's got some little piece of land that'll go under, claims he was tricked by the government or the real estate people or both but you can never tell what's what with his version of events. Anyway, I wouldn't put it past him to do some monkey business out there as well."

Norman and I jerk around in our seat belts to look at her. She looks back at us with her shrewd blue eyes glinting and her hands neatly folded over her small white handbag. I adjust the seat belt to prevent myself from being strangled. Norman stamps on the gas pedal.

"What?" I croak.

"It's true," says Norman.

Della remains silent. She nods her head up and down rapidly, making little bird noises with her teeth and tongue.

THIRTY-TWO

WE SEE THE ROADBLOCKS LONG before we reach the side-road with its large coppery-brown and white sign. DellaRex Ranch, Registered Herefords Since 1966. A young constable leans down to speak to Norman.

I blurt out, "Have you found the older man in the maroon truck, an old Ford?"

"Uhh...you'd have to speak to my sergeant about that. We'd like you folks to wait here a few minutes. Got a little problem up ahead so if you'll pull up here." He points to a line-up of three cars and a two-ton farm truck loaded with sheep. He motions another officer over to talk with us. This time Norman gets a word in first.

"Hello, Sergeant Bradley? I'm Norman Szabo. I believe Staff Sergeant Olyniuk spoke to you? I phoned the station in town about an hour ago. About this matter, here."

Sergeant Bradley scans our carload of incipient weirdos with a calculating set of pale grey eyes.

"I'm not at liberty to discuss this with you now, as I'm sure you understand. Now, one of you has a question?"

"Yes, me," I say. "I want to know if you've located Rex Westman? And is he alright?"

His eyes narrowed. "Rex. Westman. Yes?"

"He's driving a '50s Ford pickup, maroon colour. Like burgundy?" Still no expression from this stone-faced creature. He's not making this easy for me. "He was trying to intercept his brother, Ted. Ted's in the old red plane, old like 1948. He's probably your suspect in the pulp mill construction site bombing and we think he may have ideas about the dam construction site up ahead."

Finally some signs of life! The eyes narrow and the eyebrows meet in a menacing black line. This guy has a facial repertoire of Full Scowl, Blank Face and Getting Ready To Scowl.

"You have any information about where Rex Westman might be?"

"Look for a smaller river joining this one, flowing in from the northwest. Look for the truck being over the bank near some high yellow cliffs. The truck isn't far off the road, just a few metres in a clump of high saskatoon bushes." I say this with such authority that Sergeant Bradley seems to be taking mental shorthand as I speak.

"Thank you. Stay where you are," he snaps, and trots over to use the radio in his cruiser. We can hear him barking into his radiophone.

Once again we are forced to just sit, helpless and useless. "This is okay," Norman says, finally. "They've got helicopters above and highway patrols in all four directions so traffic can be re-routed if worse comes to..."

Whump! Whump! Whump! The car jiggles. There is a split-second of silence while our bones and our brains absorb the sounds and the shaking. Sadie Brown whines in pain and barks once, jamming her head into my legs, trembling uncontrollably. Norman presses his head onto the steering wheel and Della, amazingly enough, isn't making a peep. I can't turn to look at her. I stare straight ahead, as dark brown dust settles everywhere, as if a giant is sifting topsoil above us. I can just make out the flashing blue and red lights of a police cruiser heading our way. I cross my fingers and toes. The cruiser stops at the roadblock.

Rex gets out, slowly, and stands, leaning against the vehicle. Della shoots out the back door and is beside him in a few more seconds, reaching up and patting his face. They turn away from us then, hanging on to each other and looking toward the deep crease in the plateau that holds the river. The crease contains the remains of a dam site. And what's left of Ted Westman and his kamikaze planeload of explosives.

EPILOGUE

Home is not where you live but where they understand you.
–Christian Morgenstern

I THINK THE HARDY THÉRÈSE Bugnet rose will give the Whitehorse climate a run for the money. Or, more aptly, a run for the roses. If anyone can make them flourish, Francine Szabo can. People come from all over just to look at her flower and vegetable gardens and to buy transplants from her greenhouse.

Norman and Francine, as well as their fifteen-year-old twins, Sam and Bobbi, will be visiting me on their way back from Disneyland in a few weeks. Already they're as familiar as my "real" family. Norman may have something to report from his preliminary hospital and adoption records research as well. He and Francine are very intrigued with Ginger and Emil's story. His parents, who I'm looking forward to meeting, took forty years to tell him he was adopted but they all survived the news.

go on, go on! tell me more!

"Ginger, if that's you, you can just cool your jets! Soon, okay?"

I'm pleased and amazed to think that I handed in four feature articles, eighteen photos, and some short sidebar stories, which include Francine's greenhouse, a pattern for husky dog booties, some terrific recipes, and instructions on how to build your own sweat lodge. *Great Northwest Expeditions* is pleased too.

Not another soul was injured when Ted Westman flew into the half-built dam, thanks to a wildcat walkout in support of the pulp mill workers downstream. Three weeks later the government called a complete halt and dismantled the dam project because they finally managed to renegotiate better terms for a massive hydroelectric project in the south. So the north and northwest rivers and valleys need not be sacrificed for the sake of "cheap" hydro sales anymore. Someone woke up and snorted the coffee in the corridors of our capital.

I'm going to go back north, to retrace Ginger's footsteps, as soon as I can get a proposal accepted. I want to drive the Dempster Highway to Inuvik as well. Not only that, the Flying Midwives have sent me a tentative schedule of births so I can accompany them if the timing is right. I've also heard about a man who operated on another man's eye without anaesthetic while a doctor gave instructions over a two-way radio seven hundred kilometres away. In 1939, imagine!

Just when I thought I was flush at last I discovered that the van needs a new rebuilt motor, a windshield, and a new exhaust pipe as well as the muffler. Sadie Brown is due for another bottle of insulin and box of needles. First, though, I want real shrimp for dinner, to make *cerviche flautas* for three Vancouver friends I haven't seen in six months. And fresh peach cobbler for dessert! I had a dream the first night I got back here, about children and dogs running along this beach, back and forth to their rowboats and tree-houses and such. I was silver-haired and beaming away at them all from my deck, drinking tea and scribbling down ideas for stories and poems. I was happy to the core of my bone marrow, in my dream. I even woke up beaming.

because you are happy and it suits you to a T, dear girl

Well. We'll see. Time to go inside for tea and to make a list for a shopping trip to Nelson. I am as content as I've ever been right this minute. Some dreams are just dreams, sweet dreams meandering peacefully along with no serious import. Maybe this dream means I should smell the roses right here at home. Have a little holiday. Be nice to myself. Yes.

I'd better build up my strength before I encounter the bright lights of town. A dog biscuit for S.B. and lunch for me. Let's see what's in this cookbook from that excellent bookstore in Whitehorse...

Campfire Bannock Recipe
2 cups flour
1 tsp salt
2 Tbsp baking powder
¾ cup milk or water
at least ⅓ cup lard

Mix well. Spread in greased, hot frying pan and tilt against rock facing fire. Or shape in rope with well-floured hands and wrap around green branch, 1″ thick in diameter. Tilt over fire and turn to brown evenly.

Nellie's Pemmican Recipe
Smoke meat (moose, deer) until it is dried. Pound it and make a fine powder. Mix it with lard, bear fat, caribou fat, moose fat or goose fat. You can add saskatoons to your taste or just leave plain. Put it outside to freeze in winter. Cover it with saran wrap in the fridge for summer. Old days people used to put it in deer hide pouches and bury it underground. It keeps for years. Real good with a cup of tea.

Hmmm. Not today. I'll whip up some canned mushroom soup with soda crackers on the side.

ABOUT THE AUTHOR

CAROLINE WOODWARD IS THE AUTHOR of *Light Years: Memoir of a Modern Lighthouse Keeper* (Harbour Publishing, 2015), *Penny Loves Wade, Wade Loves Penny* (Oolichan, 2010), *Disturbing the Peace* (Polestar, 1990), and two children's books, *Singing Away the Dark* (Simply Read Books, 2010), which has now been published in French, Korean, and Bulgarian, and *The Village of Many Hats* (Oolichan, 2012). She lives on the Lennard Island Lightstation with her husband, Jeff George, where she often works as a relief lightkeeper at this and other West Coast lightstations. In 2016, she was awarded an honorary degree by Northern Lights College for her literary accomplishments, particularly as they relate to the Peace River region of BC.